J

D0210702

# Leticia's Secret

by

## Ofelia Dumas Lachtman

PIÑATA BOOKS
HOUSTON, TEXAS
1997

This volume is made possible through grants from the National Endowment for the Arts (a federal agency), Andrew W. Mellon Foundation, the Lila Wallace-Reader's Digest Fund and the City of Houston through The Cultural Arts Council of Houston, Harris County.

*Piñata Books are full of surprises!*

Piñata Books
A Division of Arte Público Press
University of Houston
Houston, Texas 77204-2090

Cover art and interior illustrations by Roberta C. Morales
Cover design by Vega Design Group

Lachtman, Ofelia Dumas.
    Leticia's Secret / by Ofelia Dumas Lachtman.
        p.    cm.
    Summary:   Until she learns Leticia's shocking secret, eleven-year-old Rosario can't understand why adults fawn over this enigmatic cousin who does nothing but sit around the house.
    ISBN 1-55885-208-5 (clothbound). —
    ISBN 1-55885-209-3 (trade paperback : alk. paper)
    1. Secrets—Fiction. 2. Death—Fiction
3. Cousins—Fiction. I. Title.
PZ7.L13535Lf   1997
[Fic]--DC21                                    97-24772
                                                  CIP
                                                  AC

The paper used in this publication meets the requirements of the American National Standard for Permanence of Paper for Printed Library Materials Z39.48-1984.

# Leticia's Secret

# Books by Ofelia Dumas Lachtman

A Shell for Angela

## For Young Adults
Call Me Consuelo

The Girl from Playa Blanca

Leticia's Secret

## Illustrated Books

Big Enough / *Bastante grande*
(with Enrique O. Sánchez)

Pepita Talks Twice / *Pepita habla dos veces*
(with Alex Pardo DeLange)

Pepita Thinks Pink / *Pepita y el color rosado*
(with Alex Pardo DeLange)

For the girls who sang "Whispering Hope"
at Betty Gordon's funeral.

# Chapter One

By the time Rosario Silva had slammed shut the door of her locker, scurried down the crowded corridor, and out onto the sidewalk in front of Wagner Middle School, she had come to a conclusion. It was not a good day. Actually, it was a real bummer.

For starters, when she had gotten up that morning, she found that her special yellow notebook was gone. And it had her secret thoughts. Her grandmother Nina Sara, Rubén and Teresa shrugged when she asked about it. But worse than that was Mamá's news. Little cousin Leticia was arriving later that day. Even Teresa groaned. Then, because the kitchen clock had stopped, she was late to school. At school she learned that her best friend, Jenny Gregg, was still at home sick. And just now in Home Room, the new teacher, Miss Benson, who looked like a real live Barbie doll, added to the misery.

It happened when Miss Benson called the roll. She read Rosario's name and when Rosario answered, Miss Benson bent her head to one side and frowned. "Rosario?" she said. "Shouldn't that be Rosaria? Did they misspell it in the office?"

Most of the kids in the class giggled. Rosario said, "No, Miss Benson, they spelled it right."

Miss Benson tried to smile, but did a poor job of it. Just a tiny little twist at the corner of her lip. "I only asked because I thought that in Spanish girls' names ended in the letter A," she said. "Like María, and Luisa, and—"

"And Carmen!" Lalo Ortega called from the back, and everyone in the class burst out laughing. Lalo looked around proudly. "Rosario, Rosaria," he said, "a Rosario by any other name would smell as..."

Miss Benson rapped for silence. "Shakespeare?" she said in surprise. "Well, we can do without misquoting Shakespeare young man. We'll continue with the roll."

Rosario glared at Lalo. Why did he have to pick on her name to cause trouble?

Now as Rosario raced down the sidewalk, she was glad that the day was almost over. Of course, there was still her cousin, Leticia, to put up with. Leticia was nice enough, but all she liked to do was sit around. And she did a lot of that. By the time Rosario turned on to the street where she lived, she had stopped thinking of Leticia and she had slowed down. It was too hot to run. It was funny how September—just after school started—was always hotter than summer vacation.

Rosario's house was set in a deep lot shaded by elm trees. Mamá said they had bought the house because of the elms. The San Fernando Valley was one of the hottest parts of Los Angeles and Mamá hated hot weather. Right now Mamá and Nina Sara were sitting on the front porch drinking iced tea. The black and white cat, Pinto, was lying at their feet.

"You're home early," Mamá said. "There's some lemonade for you in the refrigerator."

"Good," Rosario said. "Did you find my yellow notebook?"

"No," her mother answered her. "What yellow notebook?"

That was the problem. Sometimes Mamá did not listen. She had shown Mamá her notebook and told her it was important and please not to let Rubén or Teresa get hold of it, and now Mamá said, what yellow notebook? It was not easy being eleven and the youngest in the family. It was not easy having a fifteen-year-old brother who thought he was a big man at the high school and a thirteen-year-old sister who was pretty, but who thought she was the prettiest girl in the eighth-grade. Then there was Nina Sara. Nina almost always spoke in Spanish and got pretty mad if anyone made fun of her English. Papá was okay.

"Here, Rosario." That was Nina Sara now. "Take these empty glasses into the kitchen. And rinse them. Don't just put them in the sink."

"I will, I will." She turned to her mother and said, "Mamá, why did you call me Rosario?"

"Because it's a beautiful name," Mamá replied and bent over to scratch Pinto's head.

"But it doesn't end in A, " Rosario said.

"It never has," Nina said. "Why should it?"

Rosario shrugged as she picked up the empty glasses and went into the house. When she had rinsed them, she took her glass of lemonade into the bedroom she shared with Teresa.

A few minutes later, when Teresa came into the bedroom, Rosario had all of the stuff from her clothes drawers on the floor. But there was no notebook.

"What're you doing?" Teresa asked, stepping over the pile of clothes.

"Nothing," Rosario said and began stuffing things back into the drawers.

Teresa sat on the edge of her bed. She stroked her long black hair with her fingertips before tossing it over her shoulder. "Little apple blossoms on the apple tree," she said in a sing-song way, "why are you so happy?..."

"That's my poem!" Rosario shouted. "You took my notebook!" She had a vision of jumping up and standing in front of Teresa with her hands clenched into fists, scowling at her and saying, "Look, dummy, hand it over! Now! I want it now!" Instead she stayed where she was and said, "Why do you guys pick on me? It's not very nice. You know that."

"I know that," Teresa said with a big grin. "But it's so easy." She reached under her pillow and tossed Rosario's yellow notebook onto the floor beside her. Then she got up and headed toward the door. "Anyway," she said, "you've never even seen an apple blossom!"

When the telephone rang after supper that night, it was Papá who answered it. When he was home he always did. He liked to know who was calling and why. That made Rubén and Teresa fire-engine mad, but Mamá never complained. Now Papá turned from the phone. "Mela," he said to Mamá, "it's your brother, Felipe. He and little Leticia will be arriving in an hour or so."

"How long will they stay this time?" Rosario asked.

"Be quiet, child," Nina said. "This is none of your business."

Rosario said nothing, but a voice inside of her was shouting: "It is my business! Leticia always gets my bed! And she's not so little. She's my age. Why do I have to sleep on the lumpy couch?"

Actually, when Rosario told herself, she always gets my bed, she knew that wasn't exactly true. Leticia had visited only once before and that was about six months earlier. During that visit everyone had pampered Leticia so much that Teresa got as mad as Rosario did. Only they weren't allowed to show it.

"She's company," Nina had scolded them when they complained. "And she's not used to a big city."

Today, like before, Mamá and Nina made special preparations for Leticia. Mamá put the new quilted bedspread on Rosario's bed and told her not to sit on it. And they were already acting funny. As they straightened up the kitchen, they talked softly with long, serious faces, and lowered their voices even more when Rosario came near them.

Rubén and Teresa, too, were in weird moods. Rubén, because Tío Felipe got his bed and he got a sleeping bag on the floor. And because he wouldn't

be able to stay up all night playing with his computer. Which he didn't let anyone touch. Someday, Papá
said, they'd buy one for the family, but this one really belonged to Rubén. He had won it in a contest
when Computer Circus opened up a store on
Sepulveda Boulevard. As for Teresa. Teresa was
annoyed because Leticia would be sharing the bedroom with her again, and Leticia, it seemed, had a
bad habit. She made noises in her sleep.

They were all sitting on the front porch when
Leticia and her father, Felipe, drove up in a dusty blue
Ford. "¡Hola!" Tío Felipe called as he steered the car
off the dirt driveway and under a tall elm by Papá's
pickup truck. "Here we are again, taking advantage
of your goodness."

"Not at all, not at all," Papá said as he hurried to
the car. "We're glad to have you. Eh, Mela?"

"More than glad," Mamá said, smiling. "Mi casa
es su casa, Felipe."

Rosario bit her lip. It was easy enough for Mamá
to say that "my house is your house." She didn't have
to give up her bed. Rosario was not in a good mood
as she watched Leticia get out of the car. Leticia
might not be used to a big city, but she's gotten to see
more of it than I ever have. Her father took her all
over the place when they were here before, and we
had to go to school.

Leticia ran up to her. "Hello, 'Sario," she said.

Rosario stared at her. Leticia seemed smaller than
before. Her dark eyes with the thick lashes seemed
larger than ever in her pretty heart-shaped face.

"Hi," she said finally. "Are you gonna go to school with us?"

Leticia's face turned a rosy red. "I can't," she said. "'My father's gonna take me somewhere."

"Well, good for you," Teresa mumbled sarcastically and went into the house.

"Where are you going?" Rosario asked. "Disneyland?"

"No," Leticia said. "We're just gonna see some people."

"Rosario!" Nina called. "Give your cousin a glass of lemonade and make room for her things in your closet."

"All right, Nina," Rosario said and led Leticia into the house. The screen door slammed behind them as they stepped into the living room.

Rubén growled at them as they crossed in front of the TV. "Dorks! You made me miss that pitch!"

"Sorry, Rubén," Rosario said and hurried across the room. To Leticia she whispered, "Don't mind him. He thinks he owns the place."

"That's how my brothers are too," Leticia said. "My mother says it's because they're tired."

"Tired?" Rosario asked. "Why?"

"They work in the packing house after school. They don't work in the fields anymore, not since we moved to Kelton."

"Oh," Rosario said. And because she couldn't think of anything to say about why Rubén was tired, she said, "Come on in the kitchen."

Later that night the grownups went out on the front porch to visit so that a bed could be made for Rosario on the living room sofa. It wasn't much of a bed. Just a folded up mattress pad, a couple of sheets, and a pillow on the three-cushion couch. Rosario twisted and turned, trying to get comfortable, but she couldn't spread out and she couldn't stretch her legs. She groaned. I'll lie here all twisted like a pretzel and in the morning no one will be able to unwind me. Then they'll really be sorry. That thought and the soft sound of voices floating in from the porch on the hot summer air soothed her and she drifted slowly into sleep. But her father's voice awakened her.

"Go, go!" he said firmly. "Of course, you must go!"

There was a little laugh and Tío Felipe said, "Don't send me off so fast, Jorge. There are arrangements to be made."

Rosario sat up, completely awake. What were they talking about?

"No, certainly." Papá's voice was very serious. "Stay as long as you must. But I understand your need to get back. You can't afford to lose that benefit."

"It means a lot of money, doesn't it?" Mamá asked.

"It means more than that," Nina said.

"Yes," Tió Felipe said with a long loud sigh, "there are a lot of things to be considered."

There was a shuffling of feet on the wooden floor and Nina said, "Bueno. It's time for a prayer and a good night's sleep."

When the screen door creaked open, Rosario slid under the green flowered sheet and closed her eyes. But she didn't fall asleep right away. She was thinking of what she'd heard. Whatever brought Tío Felipe here had to do with money, "a lot of money," Mamá had said. But what did Leticia have to do with it?

❖ ❖ ❖

# Chapter Two

In the morning when Rosario awakened, there was a blanket over her and the coffee table was pushed up against the couch. Someone had been taking care of her, probably Papá, and that made her feel good. Something else made her feel good. The house was filled with special smells, Sunday morning smells, of chorizo, that wonderful spicy sausage that Mamá fixed with scrambled eggs.

But when she looked in the kitchen, Mamá was fixing oatmeal as usual.

"I smell chorizo," Rosario said. "Where is it?"

"I saved you a little," Mamá said. "I made it earlier for Leticia. Remember, she's company."

"I know, I know," Rosario said. But maybe it's more than being company. Maybe everybody treats her so nicely because she's so pretty—even prettier than Teresa. "Can I have Rice Krispies with bananas instead of oatmeal?"

Mamá gave her a hug and said, "Yes, why not?"

After breakfast—and after Nina had reminded her to brush her teeth—Rosario started off for school. Pinto was curled up in a far corner of the front porch where the leafy branches of a shrub pushed through the railing and made it cool. The sun was above the treetops to the east and the morning was already hot.

As Rosario stepped out of the door, Pinto opened one weary eye.

"See you later," she called and raced down the driveway, raising dry clouds of dust as she ran. She hadn't reached the street before Teresa caught up with her.

"Wait," she called, "I'm gonna walk with you." When she reached her, Teresa said, "Leticia and her father sure left early."

"Did they?"

"They woke me up. Do you know where they were going?"

"No," Rosario said, and then they were both quiet. Rosario was thinking of what she had heard from the front porch the night before. Teresa, too, must have been thinking of something that bothered her, because there was a wrinkle between her eyes as they crossed the street.

One house down, old Mr. Milliken was dragging a trash barrel along his driveway to the street. He paused and pushed an old farmer's hat back on his head. "It's going to be a hot one," he said and yanked at the metal barrel again.

"Want some help, Mr. Milliken?" Rosario called and started down his driveway toward him.

"No, no, I hardly think so. But that's a mighty fine sentiment. Go on, scatter, girl, you'll be late for school."

Rosario caught up with Teresa. When they were one block from the school yard, Teresa said, "You go ahead. I've gotta fix my book bag."

"I'll bet you do," Rosario said. She knew it was just an excuse. She knew that Teresa thought she was too grown up to be seen with her. And it made her mad. But it also made her sad. When we went to Green Valley Elementary Teresa walked with me all the time.

Rosario stopped at her locker before going to her first class. She slammed the metal door shut and turned around, and there was Lalo Ortega. Lalo, short and chunky, had a grin on his face.

"Hello, Rosaria-a-a," he said.

"That's not my name, Lalo. You know that."

"Miss Benson thinks it should be."

"I don't care what she thinks," Rosario mumbled and headed for her class.

That day the clocks at school played games with Rosario. They moved so slowly that each class seemed twice as long as usual. And twice as dull. Maybe things wouldn't have been so bad if Jenny Gregg had been there. But Jenny was still at home getting over the flu. Anyway, Jenny wasn't the problem. It was Leticia. Where was she? What were Tío Felipe and Leticia doing? These questions kept popping up in Rosario's mind as the day dragged on. Even Team Sports, which was her favorite period, was no fun. Because it was so hot, all they did was stretching exercises. Home Room was especially boring. There were no papers to pass out, only announcements. And Miss Benson read them in a tired voice that nearly put them all to sleep. Finally, even though it seemed as if it would never happen, the last bell rang.

At home, in the kitchen, Mamá and Nina were making a special supper. They were slicing cold cooked potatoes, bright red tomatoes, and cucumbers onto a platter around cold fried chicken. And when all the vegetables were arranged on the big platter, they would drizzle them with mustardy-mayonnaisy salad dressing, and the whole thing would taste even better than the Colonel's stuff.

Nina had made a creamy pudding that had little islands of meringue floating on it. "It was too hot to bake flan," she said.

"Is Leticia back?" Rosario asked as she went to the refrigerator for a glass of milk.

"Yes," Mamá answered. "She's out in the back yard."

Rosario bit into a chocolate cookie. "Good. I'll go talk to her."

"Stay in the shade," Nina said.

Outside, Rosario found Pinto lying under camellia bushes that grew beneath one of the tall elms. But where was Leticia?

The redwood chairs on the little brick terrace that Papá had built were empty. The wooden seat of the rope swing that Teresa and she still fought for, too, was empty. Rosario stared at a far corner of the back yard that was overgrown with tall mock orange shrubs. Behind them in the cool shade was a bench she had built with bricks and a wooden board. This was her secret place, and she just bet that Leticia had found it.

Rosario ran across the yard. Carefully, she moved the branches that concealed her hideaway. She was right. Leticia was sitting on her bench, her back against the brick fence. Rosario drew in her breath. It's even worse. She's found my yellow notebook and brought it here to read!

"Put that down! It's mine!" Rosario shrieked.

Leticia jumped a little on the bench and looked around her. "What? What? What's yours?"

"My notebook. And this place. It's all mine!"

"Not this," Leticia said, pressing the spiral-bound book against her chest. "I bought this back in Kelton. It's mine."

Rosario could see now that she'd made a mistake. "It looked just like mine," she mumbled.

Leticia stood up. "If you'll get out of the way," she said, "I'll go."

Rosario didn't know what to say or do. She stared at her dusty sandals and at her big toes that were wiggling the way they always did when she was nervous. Finally, she said, "You can stay...if you want to. I made that bench. And I have a secret mail box. One of the bricks in the fence is loose and..." She stopped. She really wanted to say she was sorry.

"I'll stay," Leticia said, sitting down again. "I like this place. It has a special feeling. The birds seem to talk to you. I'll bet that at night even the stars would send you messages."

"I know, I know," Rosario said with wonder because she had felt the same thing too.

"If this place was mine," Leticia said, "I'd call it 'The Aerie.' You could pretend it was an eagle's nest far away, high on the face of a stone cliff."

"I guess I could," Rosario said, feeling more and more uncomfortable. I wish I'd never yelled at her.

As Leticia sat leaning against the cement block fence, her long black hair spilled over a pink sleeveless top and she looked like a princess in a fairy tale. Rosario bit her lip. Maybe I should let my hair grow. But it's curly. It would never look like Leticia's. And who am I kidding? It's not just long hair that makes people pretty.

"Your bench is nice," Leticia said. "Can't we both sit on it?"

"Don't know why not," Rosario said, sitting down. "This is a pretty thick board." A little brown bird stared down at them. Rosario stared back. Finally, she said, "I have a yellow notebook, too. I write all sorts of things in it. Even poems. Sometimes Teresa laughs at them."

"I wouldn't want anyone to read what I write," Leticia said.

"Why? What do you write?"

Leticia looked up at the leaves and the patches of sky that showed through them. The dry leaves rustled as the little brown bird flew away. "Mostly I write what I can't talk about," she said.

"Oh. Like what you're doing here? And why your father's here, too?"

Leticia turned on the bench to look at her. "Not really," she said. "Anyway, I don't want to talk about it. Guess I'd better go." She got up, pushed aside the branches, and disappeared.

Rosario stared after her. What did I do now?

That night they had supper on the picnic table under the elms. Because Leticia and Tío Felipe were there, it felt like a party. There were gallons of iced tea for the grown-ups and lemonade made from the lemons that grew on their own lemon tree.

Rúben was acting like a big shot, maybe because Tío Felipe was there. All he talked about was his computer and something called "e-mail" that he absolutely had to have—everyone did. Finally, between huge bites of cold chicken he said, "A nice cold beer would go great right now, wouldn't it?" And the look Papá gave him told Rosario that her brother wasn't going to mention beer at the table again for a long time—if ever.

Mamá's cold chicken platter was as good as Rosario had expected it to be, and everyone ate as if they really enjoyed it. Except Leticia. She picked around the serving on her plate, chewing the few things that got into her mouth without any enthusiasm. But Mamá and Nina kept offering her some of this or some of that. Nina even went into the house and warmed some corn tortillas for Leticia because everyone knew she liked them. You would have thought she really was a princess.

The next morning when Rosario awakened, Leticia and her father were gone once more.

"Where do they go?" Rosario asked her mother.

"I don't ask impolite questions," her mother said. "And neither should you."

School had a bright spot that day. Jenny Gregg was back! The freckles on Jenny's nose seemed darker because her face was paler, but except for that, she was just the same. Her short red hair was tousled as usual and her clear blue eyes sparkled with mischief. She sat in their first-period Math class making faces at Rosario across the room until Mr. Peters asked her if the flu had left her with a twitch. Jenny said, yes, and did he know anything she could do about it?

It was pizza day in the cafeteria. The line was long, but that didn't bother Rosario. Whenever Jenny was around, there was always something to do. This day they spent their waiting time giving names to the food on display behind the clear plastic guard. Hamburgers were Yukburgers and the green cubes of jello they named Slime Ahoy. The soup, of course, was Toxic Waste Dump. They were so busy breaking up with laughter that they almost missed Lalo when he cut into the line ahead of them. Almost.

"Hey, creep!" Jenny called. "You. Lalo. Go back to the end of the line where you belong."

"Not me," Lalo said with a little shuffle of his feet. "I know where I belong and this is it."

"Go on, get out of here," Jenny said and gave him a little shove.

Lalo said, "Cut that out!"

And the next thing Rosario knew, Mr. Márquez, the vice-principal, was there, a hand on Jenny's shoulder. But he was looking at her. "I'm surprised at you, Rosario, getting involved in a lunch-line brawl."

"No...no...I wasn't..." Rosario stammered, her face getting hot. "That wasn't..."

"As for you, Jenny," Mr. Márquez mercifully interrupted, "you'd better learn to contain your temper."

"Aw, leave 'em alone, Mr. Márquez," Lalo said with a saintly smile. "I wasn't gonna report them."

"You what?" Jenny's eyes were flashing fire.

"All right, all right," Mr. Márquez said. "Let's leave well enough alone. Lalo, move up a couple of places, and girls, behave yourselves."

"We were," Rosario said, and Mr. Márquez just shook his head slowly and walked away.

When they had found a table, Jenny said, "I'm gonna fix that Lalo, 'Sario. I swear I am. All the time I was home, I was thinking of ways to get him. The last day I was here, when I was feeling so sick, he smeared jam all over the lock on my locker."

"I know," Rosario said. "I kind of cleaned it off. I'll help you get Lalo. So long as we don't break a lot of rules. You know me, I'm chicken."

"You are not chicken. You just have better sense than some of us."

In Home Room, Miss Benson stumbled again when she read Rosario's name and Lalo laughed out loud. This time he was the only one. Rosario turned to whisper, "Sh-h-h," but Lalo was suddenly quiet. He shrugged and looked around the room with a silly grin on a face that was slowly turning red. Miss

Benson frowned and stared at Lalo for a moment, and then went on with the roll.

After school, Jenny and Rosario met by the flag-pole and started off for home. They had walked two short blocks when Rosario discovered that Lalo was tagging after them.

"Go away!" she shouted over her shoulder. "Stop chasing us!"

"Who me?" Lalo said. "This is a public sidewalk and, besides, I'm not chasing anybody."

"Look, Big Mouth," Jenny said, propping herself against a yellow fire hydrant, "if you're not chasing us, go on ahead of us."

"Go on," Rosario said. "We promise not to catch up."

Lalo, hands in his pockets, shrugged and walked past them.

The two girls giggled as they started walking again, pacing themselves so as not to catch up with him. But halfway down the block Lalo stopped and pulled off his shoe. He shook it as if to get rid of a pebble, then put it on the sidewalk beside him. Slowly, carefully, he rubbed the bottom of his foot.

"Look at him," Jenny said. "He's pretending. He wants us to pass him." She grabbed Rosario's arm. "Come on," she whispered. "We're gonna fix him."

"Sure we are. But how?"

"You'll see," Jenny said and rushed toward Lalo.

Lalo grinned up at them as they reached him, but when Jenny scooped up his shoe, the grin disappeared. "Hey! Give me that!"

Jenny said, "Ha!" as the two girls ran past him. "Give me that shoe!" Lalo yelled and hustled to his feet.

Rosario ran as fast as she could and she soon found that she was way ahead of Jenny. She took a quick look over her shoulder and saw that Lalo was gaining on Jenny. Rosario slowed down. When Jenny came alongside her, she shouted, "Hand me the shoe! I can outrun Lalo any day!"

Jenny held out Lalo's shoe and, as if in a relay race, Rosario took it and sped toward home. The sun beat down on her, but she didn't care. She loved to run. It was almost like flying. Lalo's shouts were coming closer, but she didn't care. He would never catch her. She hugged the shoe against her chest as she scurried past Jenny's corner, yelled a breathless hello to Mr. Milliken working in his rose garden, and, at last, circled the tall oleander shrubs into her own yard.

Leticia was standing on the front porch. "What's wrong?"

Rosario shook her head. "Nothing," she panted as she rushed by her into the house. She slammed the screen door, latched it, and waited, gasping for breath, for Lalo to show up.

In a few seconds Lalo, one shoe off and one shoe on, raced furiously down the driveway. He stopped dead in his tracks when he saw Leticia. He stood in a cloud of dust, his mouth hanging open. Finally, he spoke. "Wow," he said softly. "Wow."

Leticia said, "Yes? What?"

"I...you're...you're beautiful," Lalo stammered and whirled around and ran.

❖ ❖ ❖

# Chapter Three

Inside the house, Rosario sank into a chair.

Leticia came in from outside. "What a funny boy," she said. "Is that his shoe?"

Rosario giggled and told Leticia about Lalo and Jenny and what had happened on the way home from school.

"Jenny sounds like fun," Leticia said. "What are you going to do with the shoe?"

"Search me."

"He'll be coming back."

"Sure. To see you."

"No," Leticia said, her cheeks turning rosy. "To get his shoe."

"Okay then. Let's put it in a paper bag marked 'For Lalo' and put the bag at the bottom of the steps. We can hide in your father's car and see what happens."

"We can't." Leticia looked beyond the trees to the road. She looked sad. "He's gone home. But he'll be back for me on Sunday. That's only four days away."

"How come you stayed?"

"Because I had to. All right," she said in a tight little voice, "are we going to get the paper sack, or what?"

They drew a happy face on the bag under the letters that said, 'For Lalo.' Then they put it on the bottom step and scrambled into the house to wait.

It wasn't long until Lalo peeked from behind the oleander shrubs. His feet were bare and, after another glance, he walked cautiously toward the house. Halfway there he stopped and looked around once more. When he saw the paper bag, he started toward it. He bent over as he ran, like a soldier in war movies, and Rosario giggled and nudged Leticia. But she was nudging air. Leticia had moved from the window to stand at the screen door.

Lalo was at the steps. He looked in the bag, straightened up, and saw Leticia. "I...I...it's my shoe," he said.

"I know."

"Okay," Lalo said.

Rosario scrambled to her feet and to the door. She opened it, and Leticia and she stepped out on the porch. "Hi, Lalo," she said. "This is my cousin, Leticia. Lalo's the boy I've been telling you about, Leticia. He's the one who messed up Jenny's locker and who was chasing..."

Rosario stopped. There was no sense in going on. Lalo had picked up the sack and was walking away. When he reached the sidewalk, he threw Rosario an angry glance and then disappeared around the oleander bushes.

The two girls smiled at each other and then burst out laughing.

"I'll bet Nina made lemonade," Rosario said.

"Good," Leticia answered. "Let's take the lemonade and our notebooks out to The Aerie.

Outside, Pinto sat in the center of the patio washing his face. When the screen door slammed, he turned to look at the girls. Then he yawned, smoothed a whisker into place with a swipe of his paw and padded daintily away.

The Aerie was like a nest, Rosario thought as they settled themselves on the bench. They bent over their notebooks silently until Leticia said, "Why does Teresa call you 'Apple Blossom'?

"Because she found a poem I wrote. About apple blossoms."

"Could I hear it?"

"Maybe," Rosario said. "Sometime." And then, "Okay, I guess." She turned a couple of pages in her book and, after taking a deep breath, started reading.

> *Little apple blossoms on the apple tree,*
> *Why are you so happy as you always seem*
>   *to be?*
> *Is it because the sun shines on your petals*
>   *of fragrant white?*
> *Or is it because everyone loves you at first*
>   *sight?*
> *Won't you tell me so that I can be happy*
>   *too.*
> *And everyone will love me as everyone*
>   *loves you?*

Leticia said, "That's beautiful. Teresa shouldn't laugh at that."

"That's what I think," Rosario said with a grin. In a moment she asked, "What did you write today?"

"Nothing," Leticia said, "nothing really." She bit her lip and shook her head a little. "But I'll read you something I wrote a while ago. It's about how I like Kelton, the new town we live in. Here it is:

'In Kelton it's hard for my mother and father to make enough money for us since my mother doesn't have a job here. But I like it. In Smithville, the trailers we lived in, lined up like shoe boxes on a shelf, were small and ugly and the fields of beets and garlic went on forever. There wasn't even a town close by, and the TV pictures we got were fuzzy. The only excitement was on the days that the little airplanes flew over the fields, spitting out white stuff. Crop dusters. Sometimes our school bus would stop to keep out of the pilot's way and the pilot would wave at us. Kelton is different. It's a real town with a nice school and a movie house. My father says we'll get used to the trains rattling by our house. That we'll soon be able to sleep right through them. And he's right. It is getting better.'*

"I guess that's enough," said Leticia.

Rosario said, "No wonder you like to come to a city like Los Angeles."

"It's awful big," Leticia said, "but I guess it's all right."

"Don't you like it?"

"I guess," Leticia said. "I'm going inside now." She got up, pulled the branch aside and left The Aerie.

Rosario stared at the branches that were still moving. She shook her head. Well, whatever it is I do, I did it again.

At school the next day, Lalo went out of his way to avoid Rosario. He was in three of her classes and his locker was across the hall from hers, but there wasn't a word or a look from him sent in her direction. In English, when he was called on and didn't know the answer, he didn't make a wise crack. Instead he said, "I'm sorry, Mrs. Wilmer, I don't know." Mrs. Wilmer pushed her gold-rimmed glasses up on her nose and gave him a puzzled look. In the back of the room, Honey Chávez cracked her gum and muttered, "Jeez, Lalo must be sick or something."

At lunch, Jenny whispered, "Boy, is that Lalo acting strange. I guess we really got to him with the shoe business."

"We didn't get to him," Rosario said, shaking her head, "I think Leticia did."

"What'd she do?"

"Nothing. She just stood there. And so did Lalo. Then he said something silly and turned around and ran."

Jenny grinned. "That Leticia must be something. I've gotta meet her."

After school, Jenny telephoned her mother. When she was through, she ran out to Rosario, who was waiting by the flagpole. "It's okay," she said. "I can come to your house. My mom says it's okay so long as I'm home by five."

On the way home Rosario looked over her shoulder a couple of times. Jenny did too. But Lalo didn't chase after them this day.

As usual, Mr. Milliken was working in his garden. "Rosary," he called, his wrinkled face breaking into a broad smile, "come here. I've cut some roses for your mother."

Jenny nudged her and whispered, "Why does he call you that?"

Mr. Milliken waved a trowel at Jenny. "Because I like to," he said. "And don't think, young lady, that because I'm an old man I can't hear."

Jenny shrugged.

Rosario said, "Mr. Milliken always calls me that. When we moved here, he asked me what Rosario meant and I told him, 'rosary.' And then he asked if he could call me Rosary, and I said, 'Sure, why not?'"

Mr. Milliken grinned. "And Rosary she remains until she tells me otherwise. And then, perhaps, if it befits her, I will call her Rosario."

"What does that mean?" Jenny asked.

"Someday Rosary will know," Mr. Milliken said. From the ground by his feet he picked up a bunch of paper-wrapped roses and handed them to Rosario. "Go on, scatter, girls. It's too hot for all of us here in the sun."

"He's strange," Jenny said.

"No, he isn't. He's just kind of...kind of...literary. Come on."

They left the roses with Mamá in the kitchen and went into the back yard to look for Leticia. They found her sitting on a redwood chair in Papá's patio.

"You're not a blonde at all," Jenny said to her. "For some reason I thought you were a blonde."

"Me?" Leticia said. "Well, I'm not. But you're a redhead, all right."

"Down to my freckles," Jenny said. "Hey! Why don't we walk down to 'Yo, It's Yogurt.' They've got a new flavor called Raspberry Riot."

"Want to?" Rosario asked.

"I don't think so," Leticia said. "I just thought I'd sit around." Then, with a sparkle in her eye, she added, "I found your mailbox, 'Sario. Go look in it."

Jenny raised her eyebrow in a question, and Rosario said, "In The Aerie. My special place. Come see."

"It's neat," Jenny said once they were inside the shadowy corner. "Really neat. And cool." She plopped down on the bench. "How come you haven't shown it to me before? I thought I was your best friend."

"You are. Sure you are. But this was going to be my secret, and then Leticia found it."

"Oh. Oh, well. Where's the mailbox?"

"Here," Rosario said, "here in the corner. One of these half bricks is loose and..." She tugged at the brick and it turned slowly, as if it was on a rusty hinge. "Look. An envelope."

"Well, open it."

Rosario tugged at the envelope and pulled out a photograph. "It's a picture of Leticia. It says, 'To my cousin with love, Leticia'."

Jenny took the picture and looked at it for a little while. "Whoever took this really knew about cameras," she said. "My dad says portraits are real hard to do. Gosh, she's pretty."

"Yeah, I know."

Jenny stared at the photograph. Suddenly she jumped up. "Ha!" she said, waving the picture in front of her. Then she lowered her voice. "You know what you were wondering about? What Leticia and her father are doing here? Well, I've got it! She's trying out for the movies, or for TV commercials."

"Uh-uh," Rosario said, shaking her head. "That's a dumb idea." And then, "Do you really think so?"

"Sure. I'll bet that's where she goes with her father."

"I don't know, Jenny. How would she know about movie studios, or TV places, or anything? She comes from a tiny little town."

"Doesn't matter. She might have won a magazine contest or something. You know, for a movie tryout."

"Maybe," Rosario said. "I guess it could happen. I did hear my mother say that their coming here had to do with a lot of money."

"See?" Jenny said triumphantly.

Rosario peeked through the branches across the yard to where Leticia was still sitting in the patio. Her cousin was pretty enough for a magazine cover. Maybe that's why Mamá and Nina pamper her so much. Because someday she might be famous.

Jenny was still looking at the photograph. "This is probably a copy of the picture they sent in to get the first interview."

"You mean like when they were here six months ago? That could have been for tryouts?"

"Sure," Jenny said. "And now they've called her back. But they've sworn her to secrecy."

Rosario nodded slowly, a frown on her face. "I suppose it could be," she said. "Whatever it is, she sure doesn't ever want to talk about it."

"Of course not," Jenny said. "She doesn't dare mess up her big chance."

"'Sario," Leticia called from the other end of the yard, "did you find it?"

"Sure," Rosario said. "We're coming." She pushed the loose brick into place and followed Jenny across the back yard.

When they were all sitting on the patio, Leticia said, "Will you give me a picture of you?"

Rosario frowned in concentration, then shook her head. "I don't think I have one, except with the whole family."

"I know what," Jenny said. "Tomorrow I'll bring my camera over and we'll take pictures of all of us."

"Would you really?" Leticia said. "That sounds like fun."

"You bet I will," Jenny said and gave Rosario a sly wink. "Right after school. My dad says I'm pretty good with the camera."

Leticia stood up. "If you guys don't mind, I'm going in now. I've got something to do." They watched her walk gracefully around the patio, across the yard and up the back steps.

Jenny shook her head slowly. "She's nice," she said, "but she's really kinda funny."

When Jenny left and Rosario went into the house, she discovered that Leticia had gone in to read. She was lying on the bed, right on top of the new quilted bedspread, reading "Little Women." Rosario decided she'd never understand her cousin. Leticia liked Jenny; she was sure of that. But she'd left anyway. If she'd gone inside to watch a favorite TV show that might have made some sense. But a book. She could read a book anytime. Oh, well, like Jenny said, she was nice but kind of funny.

❖❖❖

# Chapter Four

After school the next day, they took pictures in Rosario's back yard.

Leticia had on her sleeveless pink knit top, and today she had tiny pink pearls in her earlobes.

"Hey, I love your earrings," Jenny said.

"Yeah," Rosario mumbled. "She has pierced ears. Wish I did."

"Me too," Jenny said. "But right now, let's take some pictures."

Jenny took two pictures of Rosario alone, one in the middle of a laugh and a serious one. Then they took turns taking pictures of each other. Finally, Mamá came outside and took pictures of the three of them near the shrubs that hid The Aerie.

Leticia said, "I hope they're ready before I leave on Sunday."

"Me too," Jenny said, "but who knows?"

"I can mail them to you," Rosario said.

"No," Leticia answered. "Just keep them for me. I'll be coming back soon."

A look flew between Jenny and Rosario. Jenny said, "Aren't you missing a lot of school?"

"Yes," Leticia said, "but my father talked to the principal. It's all right if I do."

It looked as if Jenny would ask more questions, but Nina came to the back door and called Rosario.

Rosario ran up the back steps. "I have milk and cook-ies for you girls," Nina said. "Do you want them out-side?"

"For us, Nina? That's nice. Wait. I'll ask them."

They ended up on the front porch with their glasses of milk and plate of cookies. They finished the milk and cookies all the while laughing at Jenny's stories about Mr. Márquez, the creep, and the awful, horrible, make-you-throw-up garbage that the school cafeteria put out and called food.

"But I thought you liked pizza," Leticia said.

"When it isn't covered with yuk," Jenny said.

They were quiet for a while. Rosario was just thinking it was kind of nice to be quiet on a hot day when Jenny spoiled it all.

Jenny squirmed around on her chair to face Leticia and said, "We know why you come to Los Angeles."

"Jenny!" Rosario cried. "Why did you do that?" She was going to say more, but the look on Leticia's face stopped her.

Her cousin's pretty face was pinched into a frown and she was sitting up stiffly in her chair. "You're not supposed to know," she said in a strained little voice. "Who told you?"

Jenny said, "Nobody told us. We figured it out by ourselves."

"Oh," Leticia said and sank slowly back into the chair.

"We won't tell anybody," Rosario said quickly. "Honest we won't."

"Not until you say we can," Jenny added. "I think it's the movies and 'Sario says, TV. But maybe it's both."

Leticia took a deep breath. "Oh," she said, "oh. Maybe we'd better talk about something else."

"Sure," Rosario said. After all, this was what she had expected. Jenny, of course, was disappointed.

Rosario looked from Jenny to Leticia. The laughter and fun had disappeared. She leaned back in her chair, put her feet up on the porch railing, and stared out into the street. As she did, Lalo Ortega shot out from behind the oleander shrubs, angled past their driveway and crossed the street toward Mr. Milliken's house.

Leticia left on Sunday.

"I'll be back," she told Rosario as she got into the car. "Won't I, Papá?" she asked and Tió Felipe had nodded.

On Monday Jenny brought the photographs of Leticia to school and showed them off during the lunch hour. Rosario thought the pictures were pretty good. Jenny and she looked like two regular kids, but Leticia, all pink and white with shining black hair, looked terrific.

When Jenny told the kids at their table that she had pictures of a future movie star, a little crowd gathered around them. Even Honey Chávez was impressed by Leticia. "Boy, she's pretty, 'Sario. How come you don't look like her?"

"Because I don't," Rosario said and wished that Honey Chávez would move to Mars.

Jenny picked up the prints. "Hey, there's one missing," she said. "Who's got it?"

"Not me. Not me. Not me." No one had it. They looked on the floor and under the trays and plates on the table, but the picture was not there.

"It's one of Leticia," Jenny whispered to Rosario. "Want to bet that Lalo took it?"

"Was he even here?"

"Long enough to swipe a picture. And I'm going to get it back." Jenny walked out of the cafeteria with determination written all over her face.

When Rosario got home that afternoon, the house seemed empty because Leticia was gone. She was surprised at how much she missed her cousin. She had her bed back, and that was nice. She had her hideaway all to herself, and that wasn't. It had been fun sharing it with Leticia and calling it The Aerie.

On Wednesday, Rosario stopped thinking so much about Leticia. There was a new excitement in her life. A poetry contest!

Her English teacher, Mrs. Wilmer, seemed excited, too, as she told them about it. All middle schools in the city would be involved, she said. The winning poems would appear in a collection of young people's poetry. Only one poem would be chosen from each English class. Mrs. Wilmer nodded so eagerly between each sentence that her glasses slid halfway down her nose. "But that's fair," she ended.

"Remember, this is a citywide effort and many, many poems will be selected."

Rosario rushed home the day the contest was announced. She took her notebook and hurried to The Aerie. There, in that lovely, cool place, she was sure that she would come up with a wonderful poem.

She settled herself on the bench and wrote about brown birds and blue sky and a princess in a tower. But after two long hours, she gave up. The words wouldn't work. Besides, what was the use of working so hard when she already had a poem, one that Leticia had said was beautiful? And one she was sure Mrs. Wilmer would like.

That night, she copied out her Apple Blossom poem onto a clean sheet of paper. The following day, she turned it in. It was going to be hard to wait, but they wouldn't know until the following week which poem was chosen in their class.

At her locker that afternoon Rosario wasn't thinking of the contest. She was trying to figure out which of the Vélez twins, Mónica or Mariana, had just whizzed up to her, patted her on the fanny, and yelled, "Gotcha!" And another corner of her mind was on something she had seen on the hall floor. It was a picture in a clear plastic envelope, probably a sandwich bag, and it was being trampled by dozens of feet hurrying to lockers and the outside doors. She scooped it up and quickly slid it into the pocket of her shorts. There was no time to zip it safely in her book bag. From across the corridor, Lalo had turned from a frantic search of his locker and was staring at her.

"Did you lose something?" Rosario asked, struggling to keep a straight face.

"Forget it," Lalo said crossly. "If I did, I'll find it."

Rosario twirled the combination lock on the handle of her locker and then walked slowly toward the double doors that led outside. She waited stiffly by the flagpole for Jenny, not daring to look at the plastic envelope in her pocket. And even when Jenny came, she waited until they were a couple of blocks from the school before she drew it out.

"Look what I found on the hall floor."

"Hey!" Jenny said. "It's the missing print of Leticia! You mean Lalo didn't have it?"

"I mean Lalo *did* have it. It fell out of his locker. And what's more, he didn't see me pick it up. There were too many kids going by."

Jenny took a quick look over her shoulder. "Are you sure?"

"What if he did see me? He can't very well ask you for it. It's not his."

"Good thinking." Jenny started to pull the picture from the plastic envelope but stopped. "There's something else here," she said, digging into the sandwich bag for a crumpled piece of paper. "A bunch of scribbles. And they're Lalo's. You know how messy he writes."

"What is it? Let me see."

Jenny stopped walking and stared at the paper in her hand. A smile grew on her face."

"Jenny!" Rosario said. "Don't be a worm. Let me see it."

"I think it's a poem," Jenny said. "About a girl and a punk. Here."

Rosario took the paper. Her mouth hung open as she looked at it. "It is a poem," she said, "a poem about Leticia. And the word's 'pink' not 'punk.' It's called, 'To a Girl in Pink'. Listen."

The sun was hot, I know that now
My mood was low. That, too, I know.
I rushed past leaves of dusty green
and wilting blooms of gloomy red
and she was there, a black-haired sylph.
"Yes? What?" she said.
I stood. I stared. Words would not come.
My head was wood, my knees gone weak,
My heart implored me please to speak.
But I was numb.

"A black-haired sylph," Jenny said and giggled. "That's stupid. Do you really think Lalo wrote that?"

"It does sound pretty grown-up," Rosario said. "But that's exactly how Lalo met Leticia. Who else would know about that except me? And I didn't write it."

"Do you suppose he did it for the poetry contest?"

"Oh, no! Not Lalo. I don't think he'd want anyone to see it."

"Good," Jenny said, her eyes sparkling with mischief. "He took the picture, we'll take the poem."

"What for?"

"The contest, silly. We'll turn it in for him. They're going to print all the entries in the school paper, and I want to see his face when he sees it there."

"That's mean," Rosario said. She leaned against the trunk of a tree near the curb. She stared at the paper in her hand, wishing she had never seen it. "We can't do that. It's not nice."

"Holy-moly, 'Sario. That Lalo's been making trouble for us ever since we got to Wagner Middle, and now you want us to be nice to him."

"The whole thing's not right," Rosario said. "You know, entering a contest for someone without them even knowing it. We can't do it."

Jenny snatched the paper away from her. "Maybe you can't," she said, "but I can. I'll print it up on my dad's computer..." She stopped, then added, "But I don't have to tell you anything."

When they came to Jenny's corner, Rosario said, "Don't be mad, Jenny."

"I'll have to think about it," Jenny muttered. She whirled around and walked quickly away.

Jenny was mad. No question about it. Rosario sighed and continued walking. She was two blocks away from home. It was hot, and she was sweaty and sick and tired of the heat. The cars moving on the street beside her were all smoky and smelly and that made the hot day even worse. And when she went out of her way to walk in the shade of an elm tree, a black bug fell from its branches, just missing her head. Nothing was right. At home she ignored Pinto when he walked across the porch to greet her.

Nina noticed her mood right away. "You're missing Leticia, aren't you?" she said softly.

"No!" Rosario answered. "Leticia isn't the only thing I ever think about!"

❖ ❖ ❖

# Chapter Five

Rosario ran into her bedroom. She flopped face down on her bed. Of course she had other things to think about right now! Jenny had no business entering Lalo's poem in the contest. No business at all. And Jenny had no business being mad at her either. What had she done?

All that evening she waited for the phone to ring, hoping for a call from Jenny. And every time the phone did ring and Papá answered it, she ran in expectantly, only to find the calls were not for her. She went to bed without hearing from Jenny. The next morning, she walked unhappily to school.

In Math class she tried catching Jenny's eye, but Jenny wouldn't look her way. At lunch, she slid into a chair across the table from Jenny and said, "You didn't really do it, did you?"

"I sure did. I stuck the poem under Mrs. Wilmer's door this morning. Wait till Lalo finds out!"

"Oh, Jenny, I wish you hadn't."

"Don't wish anything. Just wait and see. We'll never have Lalo bothering us again."

Rosario frowned and said, "I wish I'd never found that old picture."

"Well, wishing can't change anything, so you might as well forget it."

Rosario ate the rest of her lunch without tasting it. Every now and then she stole a glance at Jenny, but Jenny was always looking somewhere else. Everything is ugly and mud-colored, Rosario thought as she looked around the lunch area.

After school she and Jenny met by the flagpole as usual and walked home together. On the way, Jenny did a lot of whistling and humming, but very little talking. Rosario cleared her throat a lot, but all the things she thought to say came out wrong. At Jenny's corner they each said a gloomy, "See you," and went their separate ways without looking back.

When Rosario saw Mr. Milliken digging in his garden, she walked quickly and quietly, hoping he wouldn't see her. But not only did Mr. Milliken see her, he seemed to see her mood too, because his first words were, "Hey there, Rosary, what's wrong? You look as if you just lost your best friend."

Rosario drew in her breath. Her mouth hung open. How does he know? Is he some kind of a magician?

Mr. Milliken must have read her face again, for he said, "Aha! Hit the nail on the head, did I? You're on the outs with your red peppery friend, are you?"

"I guess so," Rosario said. "She's kind of mad at me."

Mr. Milliken came to the fence and patted her arm. "Not to worry. She'll get over it. What did you do? Disagree with her?"

Rosario looked at him in wonder. Was he a mind reader? "I guess I did," she said. "But I really thought I was right."

Mr. Milliken pushed his farmer's hat back on his head and nodded seriously. "Stood by your guns, did you? You're coming along, my girl. Besides, old Red Pepper will like you all the better for it. You'll see."

"I hope so. Guess I'd better go now."

She crossed the street at the corner and hurried down the driveway to the house. Papá's pickup was parked under the shady elms. Good. If he wasn't too tired, maybe he'd sit with her on the front porch. But inside she found that Papá and Mamá were busy looking over some papers on the dining room table, and although they said hello, that seemed to be all the time they had for her.

Teresa was home ahead of her and hogging the bedroom. Her school clothes, damp and wrinkled from the heat, were lying everywhere. Teresa was at the mirror pulling her hair up from the back of her neck. And the tape recorder was playing rap music that Teresa was not allowed to listen to.

"Look, you little sneak," she said. "Don't you dare tell on me."

"Why are you mad at me?" Rosario said. "I didn't do anything." She dropped her book bag on the bed and went into the kitchen.

Nina was peeling vegetables at the sink. She turned and gave Rosario a long look. "So you're home," she said. "You look as if you need a cold drink."

When Rosario started for the cupboard to get a glass, Nina said, "Sit down, child. I'll get it for you."

Rosario watched her grandmother as she walked to the cupboard and the refrigerator. Nina brought her a glass of root beer. Rosario sipped it slowly. Finally, she said, "Nina, I'm sorry I was mean about Leticia. It's not her fault that everything's wrong. I really do miss her."

"Well," Nina said, looking over her shoulder, "that's good. Because she's coming back on Sunday."

"She is? So soon? Did they call her?"

Nina turned once more. Her forehead was puckered as if she was worried. "Call her?" she said. "What do you mean by that?"

Rosarios's face got hot. "Nothing, Nina, nothing really."

Nina came to the table and put her hands flat on it. She bent over. "Don't go digging in Leticia's affairs, child," she said. "When it's time to talk about it, you will know."

Rosario knew her face was beet red. There was something in Nina's tone that made her squirm. She stared at her grandmother's hands. The veins stood out blue on Nina's brown skin, like rivers on the molded map on the table in Geography. Finally, she looked up and said, "All right, Nina. I'm going outside now."

Except for Mr. Milliken, she thought as she escaped to The Aerie, everyone seems mad at me.

Tío Felipe's old blue Ford swept into their driveway late Sunday afternoon, raising great clouds of
dust. Tío swung out of the driver's seat and wiped his
face with a handkerchief. "It's a hot one," he said.
Leticia stepped slowly out of the car and waved at
them. Rosario thought she looked tired.

They had supper that night on the patio table in
the shade of the elms. Except for the refried beans
and warm corn tortillas, it was a cold supper: sand-
wiches of cold meats and cheese on soft French rolls
and big, thick juicy slices of cold, cold watermelon.

The couch in the living room was again Rosario's
bed. And, once more, the voices of the grown-ups
floating through the screen door from the front porch
put her to sleep.

In the morning, just as before, Leticia and her
father were gone. It was as if Leticia hadn't left at all.

Rosario rushed through breakfast. She couldn't
wait to get to school. She had to see Jenny. She had
to know if this time Jenny would be friends again.

In just a few minutes she was walking beside the
fence by the teachers' parking lot. The sand-colored
buildings of the school were just ahead of her. There
were only one or two kids on the playground. She
was early. Good. She'd be sure to catch Jenny before
class. But a voice coming over the fence of the parking lot changed Rosario's plans.

"Lalo!" It was Mrs. Wilmer's voice. "Over here, by
my car."

Rosario stopped walking. She didn't want Lalo or
Mrs. Wilmer to see her, and if she went on, she would

have to go right by them. She pressed herself into a shrub growing alongside the fence. They wouldn't see her here, and she'd wait until they went away. Through the branches of the shrub Rosario saw Lalo walk hesitantly toward Mrs. Wilmer's car.

"Hey, Mrs. Wilmer. I came early, like you said. What's up?"

Mrs. Wilmer leaned into the car and pulled out a manila folder and her purse. "As I said on the phone, it's a matter we need to clear up quickly. In a contest of this nature, we need to be exceedingly careful that no cheating occurs. Let's just walk up to my classroom."

Lalo's face fell. Rosario knew why. Talking to Mrs. Wilmer by her car was one thing. Walking beside her across the parking lot and down a long hall where his friends might see him was another. If she had been Miss Benson, the Barbie doll, he might not have minded. But Mrs. Wilmer was kind of fat and her clothes were too tight on her. And she wore bright-green eye shadow.

Lalo coughed a little bit and said, "Couldn't we talk here? I...I think I'm gonna have to go to the bathroom pretty soon, so if..."

"Of course, of course," Mrs. Wilmer said hurriedly and pointed to the manila folder. "This is what I want to talk to you about. Your entry."

"My what?"

"This poem. The one you entered in the contest. I'd like to know if you wrote it."

Lalo's confident face changed. His jaw dropped and a wave of red flooded his cheeks. "Could I see?" he said and leaned over the manila folder. When he straightened up, he was biting his lip. "I didn't put that in the contest. Somebody's playing a dirty trick on me."

"Now, why would anyone do that?"

"I don't know and I don't care," Lalo said angrily. "All I know is I didn't enter any dumb poetry contest. Somebody else did it."

Mrs. Wilmer nodded thoughtfully. Finally she said, "On second thought, that does make sense. You're not the kind of a boy who wants to win a poetry contest, are you?"

"No," Lalo said quickly. "That's not my thing."

"Yes," Mrs. Wilmer said, nodding some more. "It's undoubtedly a prank. I'm relieved to see you're not claiming that you wrote this."

Lalo, Rosario decided, was about to cry. That's how he looked as he bent his head and scuffed the ground with the toe of his shoe. "I didn't say that," he grumbled.

"What? Didn't say what?"

"Nothing." Lalo took a deep breath. "I guess... no, nothing."

Mrs. Wilmer pushed her purse strap more firmly on her shoulder. She tapped the folder in her hand. "All right. This is not your poem. This is not an entry for the contest. And you had nothing to do with it. Correct?"

"Yeah."

"Well, I'm glad it's settled."

"It's not settled for me," Lalo said. "I've gotta get the creep that pulled this stunt."

"Leave well enough alone, Lalo," Mrs. Wilmer said and walked briskly toward the school building. When she was gone, Lalo slumped against her car.

Rosario waited for him to leave. But he remained leaning against the side of the car, every now and then shaking his head. When he was still there after a few minutes, Rosario began to worry that she'd be late. Finally, she started to walk, hoping hard, really hard, that Lalo wouldn't see her.

❖ ❖ ❖

# Chapter Six

But Lalo did see her.

"Rosario!" He stamped over to the wall. "It was you," he growled at her. "You're the one who found my poem. You're the one who turned it in."

"Not me," Rosario said. "I found Leticia's picture, that's all."

"Not all," Lalo said. "You found my poem, too."

Rosario felt her face getting red. "Not...not...not exactly," she stammered. When would she learn to be more self-confident, like Jenny? "Anyway, I didn't turn it in."

"Yeah. But you know who did."

"I don't want to talk about your old poem anymore."

Lalo kicked at a pebble on the asphalt and sent it flying across the parking lot. "No one was supposed to see it," he muttered.

"No one? Not even Leticia? Didn't you write it for her?"

"No!" Lalo roared. He reached in his pants pocket, pulled out a pair of mirrored sunglasses and put them on. "Tell your friend, Jenny, I'm not gonna forget this," he said and walked away.

Rosario stared after him. He thinks he's pretty cool and tough, but that poem says he's not. He was really hurt by what Jenny did.

She waited impatiently by the fence for Jenny, certain now that she was going to be late. During that short wait she made a decision. If Jenny wanted to be friends, fine. If Jenny wanted to be mad, well, not so fine, but she wouldn't do anything about it. No way would she coax her, even if without Jenny nothing would be much fun.

When Jenny showed up, Rosario could see that she was anything but mad. Jenny smiled a big smile and ran the last few steps toward her. "I couldn't wait to get here," she said. "I wonder if Lalo knows yet."

"He knows all right," Rosario said and told her what had happened. "You'd better watch your step," she finished. "He's after you."

Jenny shrugged. "I'm really worried—not! One bad word from him and I'll plaster his poem all over the school. With his name on it."

"You wouldn't!"

"'Sario," Jenny said with a quick shake of her head, "you know I would. And I'm gonna tell him so."

"I don't want to be around when you do. There's bound to be an explosion."

"I don't care." Jenny handed her a sheet of paper. "Here. I made a copy of his poem for you. So you can show it to Leticia."

"I couldn't do that."

"Why not? It's all about her, isn't it?"

"Sure. It's just that...that it's about Lalo's feel-ings...I guess I wouldn't want anyone showing my feelings around."

"Holy-moly," Jenny said. "Who made you his fairy godmother?"

Rosario laughed and put the poem in her book-bag. "And who made you the ugly stepsister?" She was going to say more, but the bell rang. They ran as fast as they could to their lockers and just made it to their first-period class on time.

Nothing happened during the rest of the school day that could be called an explosion. Lalo hung around with his usual friends, Gordito Serra, Pepe Fuentes and Johnny Cuevas, acting as if he was on top of the world. But, whenever Jenny and he were in the same room, he sent Jenny looks that were fiery enough to burn. Once, when Lalo sent one of those looks her way, Jenny actually ducked.

It was good to be friends with Jenny again. On the way home that day nothing bothered Rosario. Nothing, except for the copy of Lalo's poem in her book bag. Should she or shouldn't she show it to Leticia? First she thought, yes, and then she thought, no. Finally she decided that the best thing to do was to forget she had it.

But she couldn't. Because it kept creeping into her mind in all sorts of sneaky ways. Like, how would it feel to be so pretty that a boy fell in love with you just like that? So pretty that maybe the movies were grab-bing you up? So pretty and so likeable that every-one—except maybe Teresa—ran around trying to be nice to you? "I'm jealous, jealous, jealous," she muttered to herself as she walked beside Mr. Milliken's fence. "And that's bad, bad, bad."

"Whoa, there, Rosary!" Mr. Milliken's hand appeared above the top of the fence, waving a muddy trowel. He pushed up from the ground. "Having an argument with yourself?" he asked.

"No," Rosario said. "Just kinda talking."

"Sounded like an argument to me. Is something bothering you?"

"I guess so." Rosario's face wrinkled into a frown and she said, "Could I ask you something?"

Mr. Milliken nodded. "Shoot."

"How can it be that if you like someone, you can be jealous of them, too?"

Mr. Milliken took a crumpled handkerchief from his pocket, pushed back his hat and wiped his forehead. "Ah-h-h," he said, "deep stuff. Red Pepper again, eh? You'd like to be more like her."

"Uh-uh. Not Jenny. Well, maybe I'm a little bit jealous of Jenny, but mostly I'm thinking of my cousin, Leticia."

"I see. The little black-haired beauty. So you like her, do you?"

"She's real nice."

"That's good. Stop worrying, Rosary. We're all envious of someone or other. Anyway, no matter how hard you wish it, you can't be anyone but yourself. And, maybe, down deep, your little cousin wishes she were you."

"Me? Why?"

"Why not? Maybe there's something about you that she particularly likes." He nodded seriously and then broke into a smile. "Go on, scatter, young lady. I've got more weeds to pull."

Rosario found Leticia sitting in the patio, a book in her hand. "Hi, Leticia," she called, but Leticia didn't answer. She was asleep.

Rosario tiptoed to a chair across from her. She wanted to wake her, but decided against it. Soon Leticia started to make noises: little mutters and moans. And then she shuddered. Rosario jumped up and gently shook her cousin's shoulder. "Leticia, wake up. You're having a bad dream."

Leticia pushed Rosario's hand away. Her eyes were still closed. "I'm going now," she mumbled. "I don't want to come back again."

Rosario took a step back. "Leticia," she whispered, "are you awake yet?"

Leticia's eyes opened wide and she sat up. "Oh. Oh, it's you," she said. "I was asleep."

"You were having a nightmare."

"No," she said, "it wasn't a nightmare. It was real."

Leticia seemed so serious that Rosario, who had opened her mouth to argue, closed it again. She changed the subject. "Do you want to go watch TV?"

"Uh-uh. It's too hot inside and Papá says I shouldn't sit in front of fans."

"It's too bad we don't have an air cooler. Tell you what. I'll go get us something cold to drink."

"That'll be nice," Leticia said.

Rosario ran across the yard and up the back steps. Now I'm waiting on Leticia, just like Mamá and Nina. Why do we do that?

❖ ❖ ❖

Later that night when she awakened on the living room couch, Rosario didn't know what time it was. The house was dark and, except for the faraway traffic noises, everything was very quiet. It was at least the middle of the night. She was sure of that because the grown-ups had gone to bed very late. Besides, very early morning had a different feeling. A kind of a breathless, waiting-for-something feeling. But what had awakened her? A rustling sound, that was it. And then she heard it again. Something was moving on the other side of the room.

She sat up. "Who's there?" she hissed.

A soft whisper reached her. "Oh 'Sario, I'm sorry. Sorry I woke you up." It was Leticia.

"What're you doing?" Rosario swung her feet to the floor and tried to see in the dark.

Leticia said, "It's too hot to sleep. I thought I'd sit on the porch."

"Don't move," Rosario whispered. "You'll trip on something. Wait till I get some clothes on. I'll come with you." She pulled on the shorts she'd set out for the next day and slid her feet into her old sneakers. "I'll open the front door, then you can see your way."

Out on the porch, Rosario said in a whisper, "You're all dressed. How come?"

"I couldn't wander around in my underwear, could I?" Leticia sat down in the nearest chair. "It is cooler outside. Could we just sit and talk for a while?"

"Not here," Rosario said. "We'll wake Mamá and Papá. But I've got an idea. I'll get the stuff off the couch and we can go lie down in the back of the pick-up."

"That'll be neat," Leticia said.

Rosario bundled up her bedding and they tiptoed down the steps and across the yard to where Papá's pickup was parked under the elms. Rosario scrambled up into the bed of the truck and spread out the mattress pad. "Come on," she said to Leticia.

"It's too high."

"Just get on the bumper and push yourself over."

"I...I can't."

"Hang on." Rosario jumped down from the truck. She helped Leticia onto the bumper, then over the edge into the bed of the pickup. It was easy to do because her cousin hardly weighed anything. "You've gotta start eating more," she said somberly. "More energy foods, like they tell us in Healthful Living. Energy foods like beans and tortillas."

"*Mañana*," Leticia said with a little laugh. "Right now, forget it."

They stretched out on their backs.

"Look," Leticia said, "look up through the branches. That star up there. See? It's moving."

Rosario laughed. "Dummy, that's not a star. That's a light on an airplane. And it's moving, all right. Maybe a thousand miles an hour."

"Now who's the dummy? Airplanes can't go that fast."

"Okay," Rosario said, "so we're a pair of dummies."

"Speak for yourself," Leticia said and giggled.

Rosario stared up at the branches of lacy elm leaves and at the patches of dark sky that showed through them and sighed comfortably. It was fun being outside. It was fun having Leticia with her. She stretched, a long, lazy stretch, and watched the light of another airplane move across the sky. Finally she said, "What did you want to talk about?"

There was no answer. She pushed up on one elbow and peered at her cousin. Her eyes were closed and her breathing was deeper. Leticia was asleep. Rosario lay back for a moment and then sat up and pulled the green-flowered sheet she'd brought out over Leticia and herself. I'll be wide awake all night, she thought as she lay down again.

But the moment she closed her eyes she was asleep. She was a baby again, and Papá and Rubén were rocking her in a cradle. "We'll just roll her out to the street," Rubén said in a deep hoarse voice, "then we'll get her going smooth and easy." And he was right, because in a moment the movement of the cradle was constant and gentle. Rosario fell into a deeper sleep where there were no dreams.

How long she slept, she didn't know, but she awakened with a start. Something was very wrong. This wasn't her bed. And this wasn't the living room couch either. She was in Papá's truck. But why were they moving? She sat up.

Ahead of her in the beam of the headlights she saw that they were traveling on a narrow country road. There were no other cars. Not behind them or in front. Where was Papá going? She twisted on to her knees, ready to pound on the rear window, but one look stopped her. There were two men in the front of the truck. And neither one of them was Papá.

❖ ❖ ❖

# Chapter Seven

Rosario scrambled down to the bed of the truck and shook her cousin's shoulder. "Leticia, wake up!" she whispered. "Wake up! Something awful's happened!"

Leticia sat up. "What're you talking about?"

"Sh-h-h. They'll hear you."

"Who? And why are we moving?"

Rosario motioned to the front of the truck. "The two men in..."

A burst of laughter from the front seat stopped her. And then a man's voice said, "That's the last of the beer. Let's stop and get some more."

"Are you crazy, Ben?" This new voice was deep and angry. "We're not stopping until we get there."

"Yeah? And how soon will that be?"

"Shut up, hear?" the deep voice said. "We're almost to Walgrove. And you'll be too busy then to ask dumb questions. Which reminds me, what was in the back?"

"Some old rags near as I could tell. I might've taken a better look if those cops hadn't cruised by."

Leticia asked, "Who are those men?"

"How do I know?" Rosario whispered. "I was asleep too."

"Well," Leticia said, "at least they don't know we're here."

"They will soon," Rosario said with a shake of her head. "We'd better do something."

"What time is it?" Leticia asked.

"What difference does that make?"

"I've got to get back," Leticia said in a desperate little voice. "Papá will be waiting."

"I know, I know. You two always go somewhere. Sh-h-h, they're talking again."

"Stop whining, Ben," the deep voice said. "This heist will go smooth as a baby's bottom. Frank and Bug will have the place open for us. We just pull up and start loading."

"Yeah, sure," the other man said. "It talks good."

"It works good too. Now shut up and let me drive."

Rosario was getting more and more frightened. If they find out we're here, who knows what they'll do. They might even kill us. She shuddered. Maybe Papá and Mamá have found out we're missing. Maybe they're coming after us right now. At her next thought she swallowed hard to keep from crying, and her heart landed like a heavy rock in her stomach. That isn't going to happen. No one has missed us yet; at home everyone's still asleep. No one's going to help us.

She glanced at Leticia. Leticia was huddled in the corner of the truck away from the rear-view window. Her eyes were closed and she was whispering softly to herself.

She's praying, Rosario thought. Maybe I'd better pray too. No. Nina prays a lot, but she always says that God helps those who act, not just ask. So if Leticia's going to pray, maybe I'd better figure out what to do.

She stared at the countryside they were passing. They seemed to be driving through thick groves of trees that hugged the edge of the road. It looked as if they weren't anywhere near a town. But the man had said that they'd soon be at Walgrove. Once they got there, it would be too late. A plan. She had to have a plan. She looked down at the road. It seemed to be sliding quickly beneath the wheels. The pick-up was going too fast to even think of jumping out. But what else was there to do?

Then from between the trees a pair of headlamps beamed onto their road and in a moment a car had turned in behind them.

"Leticia," Rosario whispered. "There's a car behind us. Wave. We've got to let them know we need help. But don't yell," she added quickly. "We don't want them to hear us."

"Or see us," Leticia said. "So don't wave your arms over the side of the truck. They'll see them in the side mirrors."

The car behind them followed closely for a few yards and then, with a burst of speed, swung to the left and passed them.

Rosario's shoulders sagged. Her chin dropped to her chest. "He just waved back," she muttered. "He thought we were just waving."

"We were just waving," Leticia said. "But he did-n't know why. Rosario, I don't feel good."

"Neither do I," Rosario said. "I'm really scared. But we've got to do something."

The road beneath them was more bumpy now and Papá's little truck rattled and groaned as they rode between the lines of trees. In the dark sky above there were more stars than Rosario had ever seen before, but she hardly noticed them. In the distance far away she heard a train whistle. She liked train whistles, but this one frightened her. Maybe it meant that they were near a town.

"Leticia," she whispered, "are you listening?"

"Yes. What?"

"We've got to get out of this truck before they get to where they're going and find us."

"I know you're right," Leticia said, "but how?"

"There's only one thing to do. The first time they slow down, we've got to climb over the back and run like all getout."

"I can't."

"You've got to."

Leticia said, "Maybe if you help me, I can get over the side, but I can't run."

"Sure you can. Everyone can."

"I'll try." It was a desperate little whisper that sent a strange feeling of sadness through Rosario. Leticia covered her face with her hands and dropped her head on her knees.

Rosario sat stiffly for a few minutes. "Okay then," she said, "let's get ready. Let's slide down toward the back on our stomachs."

Without a word Leticia flattened herself on the truck bed. Rosario pulled the sheet over the two of them. They wiggled and slid toward the back of the truck. The sheet rumpled between them and they stopped to smooth it over them again. They wiggled forward once more.

Rosario pressed Leticia's arm. "Stop!" she whispered. "Listen." What they heard was a steady, clanging sound. Then there were some loud curses from the man in the driver's seat, and the pickup came to a sudden stop.

Above the shrill clanging they heard a rumbling roar and the piercing whistle of a train. It was a train crossing!

"Leticia, come on," Rosario whispered, throwing the sheet off of them, "let's go!" Rosario scrambled out of the truck onto the road. "Come on," she whispered. But Leticia was having trouble pulling herself over the edge of the pickup.

"You've gotta help me," she said.

Rosario clambered back onto the bumper. With Leticia hanging on to her, Rosario pulled her out of the truck and down to the road where she landed on her hands and knees.

"Let's go," Rosario said and ran over the edge of the highway and into the grove of trees. But Leticia was not behind her. She was still by the truck, struggling to get up. Rosario ran back and helped her.

"Come on, run!"

"I'm sorry, 'Sario, I can't."

"Well, walk fast then." Rosario straightened up and as she did she saw the driver's head poked out of the truck.

"Hey!" he bellowed. "Where'd you kids come from? What're you doin' back there?"

Rosario grabbed Leticia around the waist. "Run!" she said. "I'll help you!"

Together they staggered off the road and into the trees. The soil between the rows was soft and crumbly, making it impossible to run. It was even hard to walk. Rosario pulled her cousin behind a large clump of bushes growing between two trees.

"Get down! Get down!" she said. We'd better hide!"

Leticia, without saying anything, fell to the ground beside her. They huddled together, breathing hard.

The bell at the train crossing beat steadily and the rumble of the train grew louder. The roar came closer and closer until it seemed that the train was racing right above their heads. After what seemed like hours—it might have been one or two minutes—the warning bell at the crossing stopped.

Leticia grabbed Rosario's arm as the sound of the train faded. "Are they coming after us?"

"I don't know. I hope not. Maybe they just want the truck."

In the quiet that followed, Rosario heard nothing but Leticia's breathing and her own heart pounding. But in another moment, she heard the familiar sound of Papá's pickup starting up. She heard it bump over the railroad tracks, and then the hum of the motor faded away. It was quiet for a brief moment and then, one by one, the crickets began their song until a chorus of cricket music filled the night.

"Are they gone?" Leticia asked.

"I think so. But let's wait a little while."

They waited. In a few minutes Rosario nudged her cousin. They got up and walked cautiously to the edge of the road. Except for a scattering of lights on a faraway hill, they were standing in darkness.

Leticia moved closer to Rosario. "Where are we?" she asked.

"I don't know. On the way to a town called Walgrove, I guess."

"Is it near?"

"How would I know?"

"Don't be mad at me, please, Rosario."

"I'm not mad. I'm ...I'm just scared."

"Me too."

At that moment, a little breeze rose and blew down the highway, whisking up the dry leaves scattered at its edges. Leticia shuddered. "What's that?"

"I don't know. Leaves blowing...I hope." Rosario looked around her. Nothing was moving...so far. She took a deep breath. "You know, Leticia, we can't just stand here being scared. Let's walk toward the town. Maybe it's near."

Leticia groaned. "I...I..."

"What?"

"Nothing," she said in a shaky voice. "I...I guess we can go."

❖ ❖ ❖

# Chapter Eight

In a very few steps they reached the train crossing and discovered a light. It was a weak yellow light that hung high above the crossing. It had been hidden by the trees. They were glad for its pale glow, because the road across the rails was rocky and uneven. They crossed the tracks hand in hand and in just a few moments they left the dim little light behind.

The air was cool and filled with the sweet smell of night-blooming flowers. Above them in the sky the stars were crowded together, some trying to outshine the others, and on the ground the crickets made music from under every bush. If things had been different, Rosario might have enjoyed it. But they were in a terrible fix, and she didn't know how, or if, they'd get out of it.

The groves of trees grew thinner as they walked. Pretty soon Leticia said, "Look! Over there on the right side. There seems to be a bench or something. Can we stop and rest?"

What Leticia thought was a bench turned out to be a couple of wooden boxes, the kind fruit is packed in. Leticia turned one over and sank down to it. "'Sario," she said, "I'm sorry but I can't walk any more."

"We can't stop now," Rosario said. "We've got to find the town."

"I know, I know, but...I just can't." Leticia's last few words were almost lost in a sob. "I'm sorry," she repeated. She buried her face in her hands and cried softly.

Rosario turned the second box over and sat beside her. "What's the matter?" she said. "Are you sick or something?"

"Yes-s-s." The word was hardly more than a breath.

"Do you need to throw up?"

"No." Again the word was almost lost in Leticia's breathing.

"Well, what is it then?"

Leticia rubbed the back of her arm across her eyes. "I'm not supposed to talk about it."

"I won't tell anyone," Rosario said.

Leticia bit her bottom lip and frowned. "Are you sure?"

"Cross my heart."

"All right then." Leticia drew in her breath and let it out in a long, shuddering sigh. "'Sario, something's terribly wrong with me. I have a very bad disease."

Rosario started to say, "What?" and then clamped her mouth shut. A dreadful sadness filled her. She looked through the darkness that separated them into Leticia's pale face. "Oh, Leticia," she said in a shaky little voice, "you have AIDS."

"Oh, no," Leticia said quickly. "Not AIDS. I have cancer."

Rosario drew in her breath. "Golly," she said, "that's awful."

Leticia nodded. "I know. They don't tell me much, but I heard the doctor talking to my father about a kind of cancer that's doing terrible things to my insides."

Rosario stared at the trees across the road. She wondered for an instant if this was really happening. She wondered if it was just part of a weird dream. But in the next instant she knew better. Leticia and she were alone on an empty country road in the middle of the night. And Leticia had just said something awful. She turned back to her. Now that her eyes were more used to the dark, she saw that Leticia's face, usually so pretty, was pinched and strained and streaked with tears.

"Maybe," she said finally, "maybe you didn't hear right."

"Uh-uh," Leticia said. "I heard right, all right. Anyhow, they're trying to help me. That's why we come down here."

"Here? To my house?" Rosario said. "To do what?"

"To get special treatments for me."

Rosario swallowed hard. So that's what Leticia and her father did. But why here? "Why all the way down here?" she asked.

"Because the hospital in Hollywood is the only one with the right machines for my treatments."

"Oh," Rosario said. Hollywood. But not for movie tryouts. Leticia came here to be treated by horrible machines. Jenny and I were absolutely, stupidly wrong.

"Are you okay now?" she asked. "Does anything hurt?"

"I'm okay. Nothing hurts yet," Leticia said. "Papá gave me my medicine just before I went to bed. But I'll need it again pretty soon."

Rosario stood up. "We've gotta do something," she said. "We've gotta do something." As she spoke a pair of headlights appeared on the road on the other side of the train tracks. "A car's coming. I'm gonna ask for help."

Leticia got up slowly and they both stood at the edge of the road, peering eagerly towards the oncoming car. When the car paused under the light of the railroad crossing, Leticia pulled back.

"It's them," she said. "They're looking for us!" She scurried away from the road and crouched behind a thicket of shrubs.

"Oh, no, please no," Rosario said and hid behind the trunk of a tree. She watched as a blue pickup truck bumped over the tracks and rolled toward them. It rattled past them and immediately disappeared at a curve in the highway.

"Leticia," she called, "that wasn't my father's pickup. It's all right. Come out."

When Leticia was sitting on the box once more, Rosario said, "That truck stopped right around that curve. I heard his squeaky brakes. And if there's a stop there, maybe there's another road and maybe it goes to Walgrove."

"Sure, maybe, but..."

"You don't have to come, but I've got to see what's there." Rosario leaned over and dragged the box she had been sitting on behind the shrubs.

"What're you doing?"

"You'll see. Just get up. We'll put both boxes back there and you can lie down on them where no one will find you. I'll go see what's out there."

"Maybe we both ought to stay here till it's daytime."

"What good would that do?"

"None, I guess." Leticia's voice was getting whispery again. "I guess it would be worse. 'Cause I'd miss my treatments, and I'm not supposed to miss any."

"Of course not," Rosario said. "You came all the way down here for them. Are you scared to stay alone?"

"Sure. Sort of. Aren't you scared to go out there alone?"

"I guess I am," Rosario said. I know I am. But if I don't find someone to help us, Leticia will miss her treatments and her medicine and maybe she'll start hurting. So I've got to go. There's nothing else to do.

"I'll be all right," she said. "You just stay hidden."

Leticia said, "Saint Christopher will take care of you."

"I hope so. Okay, see you."

Rosario followed the road around the curve. She had been right. There was a stop sign at the end of the curve where another thoroughfare crossed it. This

road was tree-lined, too, and dark and empty. It looked creepy. It didn't take her long to decide that that wasn't the way to go. She decided, first of all, that if she did she might get lost. And, besides, there had been three cars using the road she was on, which meant that it had to lead somewhere. And that settled it. She crossed the intersecting street.

As she walked, her eyes darted back and forth, looking into the trees that now seemed filled with threatening shadows. She edged away from the trees to walk in the center of the pavement. A few lights still glimmered on the faraway hill ahead of her, but below them there seemed to be nothing but darkness. When something rustled behind her, a cold chill crawled up her back and down her arms and she started to run. She glanced over her shoulder and saw a small animal crossing the road. She slowed down. She told her heart to stop racing, that it was probably a cat.

Now in the distance a dog barked. And then another. Close by, a third dog joined them with loud howls. Those dogs belong to someone, she thought. She must be near houses. She must be near the town. Ahead of her she sensed more than saw that the road curved once more to the right. Then she saw a diamond-shaped highway sign with a curvy black line painted on it. "Slow. 10 Miles," it said.

She followed the curve and stopped dead in her tracks. Two or three blocks away there was a light hanging over an intersection. There were small buildings that looked like stores surrounding the lighted corner. Tears of relief filled Rosario's eyes, and the street light danced and shimmered before her. It's Walgrove! Now I can get help!

With her heart beating with excitement she started walking again. First there were fields that were empty except for some large trees. Then, on each side of the street, the buildings began. The two to her right were dark, with large CLOSED signs in their display windows. A gasoline station with two pumps was at the first corner. She started to walk by it, but stopped, hugging the trunk of a tree. A blue pickup was moving without the headlamps on from behind the gas station into an alley. It was heading for the rear of the buildings that stretched out from the main corner. She knew that truck. It was her father's.

As she watched one of the men in the front seat jumped out and ran ahead of the truck. She kept on watching until the truck was lost in the murky shadows. Then she pushed away from the tree and ran. In a few seconds she was at the lighted intersection. She glanced at the street sign that said, Walgrove Avenue and Main Street. She turned on Main. She had to find help before they found her. But it was too late. They'd seen her!

A large paunchy man had appeared from nowhere in the middle of the block behind her. "You! Kid! Stop!" he called.

She ran faster. She was dimly aware of the stores she passed. A drug store, J. C. Penney's, and another with a huge red sign that said, RANDY'S GRAND OPENING. And then with horror she saw that beyond these stores the dark highway began again. She couldn't go out there.

The paunchy man was gaining on her. She could hear his heavy breathing and his footsteps. A sob escaped her. Dear saints in heaven! Saint Christopher, where are you? Out of the corner of her tear-filled eye she saw a narrow opening between two small buildings. This had to be a place to hide. She swerved into it. A place to hide, all right. But no way to get out of it. She was facing a high brick wall.

❖❖❖❖❖❖

# Chapter Nine

Rosario turned her back against the bricks. She was in a narrow little alley lined with trash cans. She slid behind the tallest one. "Go away!" she cried to her pursuer.

The man stopped. He filled the entry to the alley, closing her in.

"Go away!" she yelled. "Leave me alone!"

"What's the matter, kid?" the man said. "What in blue blazes are you running away from?"

"You!" Rosario shouted. "You've got my father's truck. Now leave me alone!"

"You've got me wrong, kid. I'm a policeman." He backed out onto the sidewalk. "Come out here where I can see you."

"No!"

"D'ya want me to come in and get you?"

"No," Rosario said more softly and inched along the wall of the building to the edge of the sidewalk. "Don't touch me," she said, "or I'll scream!"

"And I'll bet you would," he said with a grin. "Okay, now, don't be afraid. Just tell me. What's going on?"

Rosario stared at him. He was wearing a uniform, but it was tan not dark blue like the police wore in Los Angeles. "How do I know you're a policeman?" she said, taking a step back. "You don't have a badge or anything."

He reached in his pocket and pulled out a small leather case. "The badge is in here. But you're too edgy to come close enough to see it. So, tell you what. See that lighted window in the building across the street? That's the police station. You walk over there nice and easy and I'll follow you. But no running, hear me?"

Rosario glanced at the leather case, then at the lighted window. She nodded and started across the street. When she saw that the window said, "Walgrove Police Station," she let out her breath. Her shoulders, which had been as stiff as a ruler, relaxed. She turned and nodded once more to the man behind her.

"Go on," he said, "open the door. It's only Hal in there and he's probably asleep."

Hal, a thin young man with brown-rimmed glasses, jerked his head off a battered wooden desk as she opened the door. He stared at her with sleep-heavy eyes and then looked above her head. "What's going on, Chief?" he said to the man following her in. "Who's the kid?"

"That's what I aim to find out," the Chief replied. He turned to Rosario. "Now, young lady, who are you and what truck am I supposed to have taken?"

"Oh! The truck!" Rosario said. "Two men stole my father's pickup truck with my cousin, Leticia, and me in it. And they're using it to steal some stuff from one of your stores right now!"

The two men stared at her. The Chief shook his head. "You wouldn't be trying to spoof us, would you?"

"No! No, of course not! My name's Rosario Silva and I live in the San Fernando Valley, and my cousin and I were sleeping in my father's pickup and when I woke up we were moving and these men were talking about going to Walgrove and how two other men named Frank and Bug would be waiting for them with the store open and how they'd load up the pickup and..."

"Whoa!" the Chief said. "Simmer down. Now, where's this cousin you're talking about?"

"Leticia, that's my cousin, is hiding behind some trees on that road by the train tracks. She...she can't walk too much."

"Chief," Hal said, "Randy's Electric Alley opens tomorrow and he's got the place packed with..."

"Yeah," the Chief said, "yeah. Frank and Bug, eh? We're gonna have to see about that." He picked up the phone and punched in a number. "Florence," he said, "we have a little problem. Get over here fast. I want you to watch a kid I have in tow while Hal and I size something up."

Florence must have asked a question because he went on to say that they were checking out the possibility of a burglary in progress. Then he and Hal stood by the door. When the woman called Florence walked in through the rear door, they ran out, moving quickly and silently across the street.

Florence was blonde and plump. She was wearing tan pants and a tan shirt just like the Chief's, but on her they looked different. Besides, she had a badge pinned on her pocket. She smiled and said, "Okay, honey, what's your name?"

"Rosario. Rosario Silva."

"All right, Rosario, sit over there. All we can do is sit and wait until Jack, that's the Chief, and Hal get back."

"No, ma'am," Rosario said. "I can't just sit. I've got to get my cousin. She's hiding behind some trees and she's scared and she's sick and she can't walk very much. So I've gotta go." Rosario took one step toward the door, turned, and began to cry.

Florence handed her a tissue. "Now, now, honey, what's all this? What's going on?"

Rosario wiped her eyes and blew her nose and told her. And when she was through, Florence said, "C'mon, honey, let's go get Leticia. My car's in back."

Rosario followed Florence through a door in the rear of the room and down a long hall. There was a door at the end of the hall, but before they reached it the solid wall ended and a section of steel bars took its place.

"Is that a jail?" Rosario asked.

"Sort of," Florence replied.

Outside, they got into a police car and in a few minutes they were at Leticia's hiding place. Rosario jumped out of the car and called, "Leticia, Leticia, where are you? Come out. It's all right."

"I'm here," Leticia called from deep in the grove of trees. "I hid when I saw the lights."

Rosario went to meet her. "Do you need some help? Can you walk all right?"

"I can walk all right, but I'm awful tired."

Florence was out of the car, holding the door open. "Okay, honey," she said. "Get in, get in."

Back at the police station, Florence put three chairs together and told Leticia to lie down. Then she called Rosario's home. Papá answered the phone on the first ring. "They just discovered you were missing," Florence whispered to Rosario. After Florence explained a few things to Papá and answered his questions, she handed the phone to Rosario.

"*Mi'jita, mi'jita linda,*" Mamá sputtered. Tears filled Rosario's eyes. Whenever Mamá called her "my dear little daughter," she always felt like crying.

Then Nina and Tío Felipe got on the telephone and wanted to talk to Leticia. It wasn't until Leticia convinced them that she and Rosario were both all right that they were willing to hang up.

The door at the rear opened wide and Hal and the Chief came in. A look passed between Florence and Hal, and Hal nodded and said, "We have four guests in our back quarters."

Rosario knew what he meant. They'd caught the burglars. "Is my father's truck okay?" she asked.

"It's parked in our lot," the Chief said, "and I have the keys in my pocket."

Florence threw a worried look at Leticia. "These kids need some comfort food," she said. "Time out for milk and cookies."

A full package of Oreos was almost gone when the door to the police station opened and Papá walked in. Papá, who always wore nicely ironed cotton shirts, was in a wrinkled one, and he'd forgotten a belt for his pants. Rosario felt as limp as jelly as he hugged her. "*Mi, muchachita*," he said, stroking her hair. "My little girl."

For the next half hour Papá and the Chief talked about "bringing charges" and "penal codes." When someone said, "kidnapping," Rosario spoke up. "We weren't kidnapped," she said. "They didn't even know we were there. Not until we jumped out. Isn't that right, Leticia?"

Then there was more talk, with Tío Felipe joining in, but, finally, they were on their way home, Leticia in her father's car, Rosario in the blue pickup with Papá.

# Chapter Ten

When Rosario awakened from sleep the day after returning from Walgrove, the sun was high in the sky. She vaguely remembered Teresa tip-toeing by the couch and then Rubén searching the room for his books. And now it was Nina bending over her.

Rosario sat up. "What time is it, Nina? I'll be late for school."

"School? What is this with school?" Nina said. "You're not going anywhere today."

"I'm not? Does the school know?"

"Your mother left too early to call them, so I did."

"You, Nina?" Rosario said with a grin. "How? The lady in the school office can't speak Spanish."

"Humph!" Nina said. "I can speak English when I have to."

Rosario wanted to say, it's not really English, but she knew that Nina didn't like being teased about the way she talked. So she said, "Where's Leticia?"

Leticia, Nina said, was sleeping. She and her father had run their usual errand and on their return, Leticia had once more gone to bed. "So be very quiet," Nina said. "No television. No radio. Leticia needs her sleep."

"I know," Rosario said, and Nina gave her a long look. She wanted to say to Nina that she really knew, but she had promised Leticia not to tell.

After a bath and a breakfast that was late, even if it had been lunch, Rosario went out on the front porch. It was strange to be at home on a school day when she wasn't sick. But even more strange was all that had happened the night before. Papá said that Walgrove was only about forty miles from where they lived, but to Rosario it seemed as if she had been in a dark little town far away, like somewhere in a dream.

She stared down the driveway past the elm trees and the oleander bushes all the way across the street. She caught a glimpse of Mr. Milliken's hat as he bent over a plant near his fence, and that made her feel better. No matter where she had been last night, she was home now—and safe.

But when she thought of Leticia, a tight little sadness filled her throat. Leticia was very sick, and that wasn't right. No one should be that sick. Sure, everyone got colds, or even a broken arm like Mónica Vélez had, but not something bad, something that needed special hospitals and special machines to help you.

Her face, she realized, was screwed up into a deep, worried frown. She hurried to smooth it out. Nina always said that if a cold wind blew across an ugly face, it would stay that way forever.

There was a sound at the door behind her. She turned. Leticia stood inside the screen door, looking pale and worn but somehow even prettier.

"Hi, 'Sario," she said. "So you didn't go to school."

Rosario said, "Missing one day won't hurt anything."

Leticia came out and sat in a chair beside hers. "Nina is fixing me some lunch," she said. "I told her not to. I told her I wasn't hungry, but she said if I didn't eat, I'd be making her unhappy."

"I know," Rosario said. "Grandmothers are like that."

Leticia nodded and as she did her eyes filled with tears.

"What's the matter?"

"Nothing." And then with a little catch in her voice Leticia added, "I'm...I'm awful scared. All those important doctors and hateful medicines, and I don't feel any better. Sometimes I think I'm never going to get better."

"How can you say that?" Rosario said, sitting up to face her. "Your father wouldn't be bringing you down here all the time if all those things didn't help."

Leticia brushed a tear from her cheek with the back of her hand. "That's what I keep telling myself. But...but when?"

"Maybe soon," Rosario said. "How do you know? So maybe that's why you should eat what Nina's fixing. You're as skinny as a twig. No wonder you don't feel good."

Leticia smiled. "You heard Nina coming," she said and got up. "Okay. I'll be back later."

Before Leticia returned, Nina called to Rosario. "Go out back, girl, and water your mother's vegetable garden. The tomatoes especially," she said. "They are starting to droop."

Rosario was glad for something to do. It was kind of boring being at home wondering what the kids at school were doing. When she was through watering the tomatoes, she pulled the hose to the shady side of the yard. There she washed off the bricks on the patio and a couple of plastic chairs. Finally, she turned off the water and went up the back steps. At the door she changed her mind about going inside.

Instead, she jumped down the porch steps, one by one. Pinto was sleeping under a bush at the far end of the back yard. She raced toward him, stopping just before she reached him. Pinto stood up, stretched, then curled up into a circle with his back to her. She scrambled up onto the picnic table, then jumped from it to land on the thick wet grass. It made her feel good to run and jump and climb. But when she looked up through the trees at the blue sky, her eyes filled with tears. It made her feel sad because Leticia couldn't do any of those things.

She wanted Leticia to get well, to grow stronger, so that they could do more together. In her own kind of quiet way, Leticia was as much fun as Jenny.

Thinking that Leticia was probably back on the front porch by now, Rosario went up the side yard. Before she reached the front, she stopped. Leticia was talking to someone. "Hello, there," she was saying. "Are you looking for somebody?"

Whatever the answer was, Rosario didn't hear it. Leticia giggled. "It's okay if you're not," she said. And then, "Come on. Don't be afraid. I don't bite."

To whom was she talking? As Rosario walked around the blue-flowered plumbago bush at the end of the porch, she knew. Even before seeing him, she knew. Lalo. It had to be Lalo.

She was right. Lalo was standing at the foot of the front steps, his hands shoved deep in his pockets as he looked up at Leticia.

"Never thought you would," he said. "Bite, I mean." His face turned tomato red. "I...I...Jenny didn't know why Rosario wasn't at school, and I was going this way anyway, so..." He let the rest of the sentence hang in the air and looked around uncomfortably.

"Come sit down," Leticia said, "and I'll call 'Sario."

"I'm right here," Rosario said. "Hi, Lalo."

Lalo stayed at the bottom of the steps. "I was going by," he said, "so I thought I'd see if you were okay."

"I'm okay," she said. "Well, come up on the porch and I'll tell you why I didn't go to school. Or maybe Leticia can tell you. I'll go get us some lemonade." She paused at the screen door and glanced at Lalo as he sat down on the top step. "You do drink lemonade, don't you?" she asked.

"Sure. Whatever you've got." He turned to Leticia. "What're you reading?"

"*A Silver Summer*," Leticia answered. "It's a book my teacher gave me."

"What's it about?"

"About a little town where a girl and her brother discover that..."

Rosario didn't stay to hear the rest. She went into the kitchen.

Nina said, "A young man to see Leticia? And how could that be? Where did she meet him?"

"He's someone I know from school," Rosario said. "But he didn't come to see me. He came to see Leticia."

"And how do you know that?" Nina asked as she pushed a half lemon onto a heavy glass reamer. "You have good points, too, you know."

Rosario grinned. It had been hard for Nina to say that. She didn't give away compliments easily. "I do?" she asked. "Like what?"

"Don't squeeze me too hard, Rosario. I've said all I'm going to say."

"All right, Nina," Rosario said, smiling. "But, anyway, he came to see Leticia. I know that. He even wrote a poem for her."

"A poem?" Nina said, her eyes widening in surprise. "What a thing. I didn't know there were boys that did that anymore. Now, in my time..." She stopped, and with a twinkle in her eye said, "But you don't want to hear about ancient times. There. Get a tray and glasses. The lemonade is ready."

Outside, Rosario put the tray on the floor by Lalo. "Sorry it's not Coke or Dr. Pepper," she said, "but...well...we don't get much of that stuff around here."

"This is okay," Lalo said and picked up the cold, sweaty glass of lemonade and drank it. When he was through, he wiped his hands along the sides of his pants and looked up at Rosario. "That was a bad scene," he said. "What happened to you guys last night, I mean."

"It was awful," Leticia said.

"Yes," Rosario said, remembering, "it was pretty scary."

"Especially when you went wandering down that dark road by yourself," Leticia said. "I'll never forget how brave you were."

As she finished talking, Leticia's face turned pale. She bit her lip as she stiffened in her chair. Then she drew in a quick breath through her mouth and said, "I've got to go in now."

Lalo jumped up. "Oh. Okay. I'm going too."

Leticia moved slowly to the screen door. There she paused and said, "Don't forget that book you promised me."

"I won't," Lalo said, a look of relief showing on his face. "I'll bring it tomorrow...if that's okay."

"It's okay," Rosario said quickly and opened the door for Leticia.

Inside the house, Leticia sank onto the living room couch. "I need my medicine," she said in a little gasping whisper. "I can take it more often now."

"Nina!" Rosario cried. "Nina, Leticia needs you!"

Nina, her face showing alarm, came running. "Your medicine?" she asked, and Leticia nodded. Nina brought her a pill and a glass of cold water and helped her to her bed.

In the bedroom, Rosario and Nina put an electric fan on the dresser, so that it moved the air but did not blow on Leticia. Then they went out and closed the door.

Nina patted Rosario's shoulder. "Try not to worry too much about Leticia," she said with a long sigh. "It was too much for her, all of what happened last night."

Rosario knew better. She had seen the pain on Leticia's face. But as she looked up at Nina's face, she saw pain there too. She nodded. "I know," she said softly, "I know."

❖ ❖ ❖

# Chapter Eleven

When Rubén and Teresa came home, Nina told them to be very quiet. Teresa scowled and Rubén shrugged. Then, after complaining about cousins who had to take naps, they grabbed up food and a transistor radio that they promised to keep on low and took over the front porch. When Jenny came looking for Rosario, they were the first to tell her what had happened.

"'Sario," Jenny said when Teresa finally called her, "is it true that you were kidnapped? Was it because of Leticia? Did they really call and ask for a million dollars ransom for each of you?"

Rosario glared at her brother and sister. "Why do you guys do that?" she asked. "Why do you tell lies?"

"What lies?" Rubén said. "Besides, don't you think you're worth a million dollars?"

Rosario muttered, "Nobody asked for a million dollars. Come on, Jenny, let's go out back."

"I called at lunch time," Jenny said as they went to the patio, "but all your grandmother said was 'sleeping.' When I asked if you were sick, she said, 'no,' so I figured something weird was going on."

"It sure was," Rosario said. "Wait till I tell you."

Jenny listened to Rosario's story, her eyes wide, her mouth falling open at times.

"My gosh, 'Sario," she said when Rosario was through, "weren't you just absolutely scared? And how come you were the only one that was chased? Where was Leticia?"

"She had to stay back in the trees," Rosario said. "She...she twisted her ankle," she added and crossed her fingers behind her back because it was a lie. "But not too bad."

"Oh," Jenny said. "Where is she now?"

"Sleeping."

"Again? She sure rests a lot. She's kind of strange, isn't she?"

"No!" Rosario said loudly.

"Hey! You don't have to yell at me."

"I didn't mean to." Rosario smiled, a weak little smile. Quickly she asked, "Did they say who won the contest?"

"Yeah," Jenny said. "That's what I came to tell you. You didn't. Mónica Vélez did. With some dumb poem about her dog. But you were second."

"Second place is okay," Rosario said and realized that today the contest didn't matter that much.

Jenny got up. "I can't stay. My mom's at her computer in her office—that's what she calls the den since she got this job—and she expects me to start dinner. My dad says he's sick of takeout food, so...well, anyway, I've gotta go."

At the end of the driveway Jenny stopped and turned. "Have you seen Lalo?" she asked. "He forgot to beat up on me for taking his poem. All he wanted to know was where you were."

"Sure, I've seen him," Rosario said. "He was here before you. To see Leticia, of course."

"Yeah, that figures," Jenny said, and Rosario walked back to the house.

Rubén and Teresa were still on the front porch. "Hey, little sister," Rubén said, "what's really going on? Tío Felipe told us some wild story, but he's always making up crazy stories. Where did you guys really go last night?"

Teresa smiled her best know-it-all smile. "You didn't go anywhere," she said. "That's what I think. Because Leticia was asleep when I went to bed and she was still sleeping when I woke up in the morning."

"They went somewhere, all right," Rubén said. "I heard them all come in this morning. But where? And why? Come on, Rosario, where'd you go?"

"Why are you asking me? Tío Felipe already told you."

"Stolen trucks? And crooks? And you and Leticia in the middle of it all? Come on now, you don't expect your big brother to believe that, do you?"

Rosario fought back tears. Why were they so mean? She took a deep breath, straightened her shoulders, and said, "Believe what you want. Or don't believe anything. I don't care." She swung around and ran along the side of the house to the back yard.

At school the next day, it was clear that Jenny had spread the story, including the million dollar-ransom stuff. Lalo must have talked about it, too, because every time Gordo Serra and Pepe Fuentes saw her, they called, "Hey, hey, Wonder Woman!" Mrs. Wilmer said, "We're glad to have you back safe and sound, Rosario." So even the teachers had heard. Even so, it was good to be back at school. Good to look at the bulletin board and see her poem posted there. Good to have other things on her mind besides Leticia. And by the end of the day, the questions about "the kidnapping" had pretty much stopped.

But the walk home with Jenny was uncomfortable. Jenny kept asking questions about Leticia that sounded as if she had given up the idea of Leticia in the movies or TV. Questions like, "I wonder what else she might be coming to L.A. for?"

All Rosario could answer was, "I don't know." And that made her squirm because she was telling another lie. Still, what could she do? She'd promised. When she said goodbye to Jenny, she dragged her feet for the next two blocks. She was afraid that Mr. Milliken would be out in his yard, and she didn't want to talk to anyone.

Mr. Milliken was out in his yard. He was tending the roses near his house. "Hey, there, Rosary," he called. "I hear you had quite an escapade."

"I don't know," she said crossly. "What's an 'escapade'?"

"Hm-m-m," Mr. Milliken said and came close to the fence. "An escapade's an adventure, perhaps a reckless one. And you're right to be sour. That doesn't describe what happened to you, does it?"

She shook her head. "No. What we had was a bad, bad, awful experience." She smiled, sorry that she had been cross with him. "But we came out of it all right."

"So I heard. Your parents are very proud of you. They say you are a very capable girl."

"But they don't trust me." Rosario didn't know she was going to say that. She hadn't even known she was feeling that way.

"Well. And what makes you say that?"

"I don't know, Mr. Milliken, I don't know exactly. It's just that they don't treat me like a grown-up. Like I know something about Leticia that they don't want to tell me because they think I'm too young to know. And that isn't so. I'm not too young at all. Anyway, she's my cousin and I think I should know what's happening to her. Well, I do now, but they didn't tell me, she did."

"Maybe," said Mr. Milliken, "maybe they don't want Leticia to be hurt. Isn't it possible that if you all knew Leticia's secret, someone, even you, might say or do something that would hurt her? Not on purpose, of course. Sometimes even too much kindness can be hurtful."

Rosario stared at him. "Mr Milliken," she said, "you know about Leticia, don't you?"

"Yes," he said with a sad smile. "Your uncle and I have had some long talks."

"Oh."

"Your uncle doesn't want Leticia to be any more scared than she already is, and if Teresa and Rubén and you started being especially nice to her, she would really wonder why."

"Nina and Mamá baby her."

"That's different. But if her own cousins did, my, oh, my. That would really be something to think about."

"Oh," Rosario said again, because she was having trouble saying anything. She wiggled her shoulders to adjust the bookbag on her back and cleared her throat. Finally, she said, "So I shouldn't be especially nice to Leticia?"

"Just regular, I think," Mr. Milliken said. "That's how we should all treat each other."

Rosario gave him a questioning glance. But Mr. Milliken wasn't going to explain anymore. He was following the flight of a noisy blue jay from a corner of his fence high up into an elm.

"Well," she said, "I guess I'd better scatter."

Mr. Milliken grinned. "I suppose so," he said. "Time I went inside."

As Rosario walked into her driveway, she saw Tío Felipe by his car under the elm trees. She thought she would say something to him—she wasn't sure what—and took a step toward him, but stopped when she heard Leticia.

"'Sario," she was calling from the front porch, "we're waiting for you. I'm going home. I don't have to come back any more."

"Really?" Rosario hurried up the steps. "I'll bet you're glad," she said as she dropped her bookbag on a chair.

"Sure. But I'll miss you."

"I'll miss you too," Rosario said. "I'll write to you."

Leticia glanced toward her father's car. "Papá's getting cross. He wanted to leave this morning, but I wouldn't go without saying goodbye to you."

"Of course not. You couldn't just go."

"But I have to now. Papá's sending me looks. He says we won't get home until late tonight."

"I'll think about you a lot, Leticia," Rosario said. "Especially when I'm in The Aerie."

"Me too." Then, with a little smile, Leticia added, "I have an idea. Every day at four o'clock let's pretend we're together in The Aerie. I'll go to a quiet spot and you'll go to The Aerie and we'll pretend to talk together."

"That's cool!" Rosario said. "We'll send each other mental messages. Let's start tomorrow."

At that moment, Nina and Rosario's mother stepped out onto the porch.

"Well, you finally got here," Mamá said, patting Rosario's shoulder. "Leticia has been waiting patiently, and your uncle not so patiently, for your return."

Leticia said, "Goodbye, 'Sario. Maybe you'll come up to Kelton and visit me."

"Maybe," Rosario said, suddenly all tight and hurting inside. "Maybe."

Leticia walked slowly down the steps. At the bottom she turned and waved.

In another minute, Tío Felipe's car was swinging into the driveway. Leticia leaned out of the open window. "Four o'clock," she called. "Remember!"

"I'll remember," Rosario said. "I promise."

❖ ❖ ❖

# Chapter Twelve

Two surprising things happened in the hour that followed Leticia's leaving.

The first was that Lalo came over with a book for Leticia...and stayed.

He didn't ring the doorbell. Instead he called, "Hello?" through the screen in a questioning voice.

Rosario went to the door and said, "Oh, Lalo, I'm sorry, but Leticia had to go home."

"She did?" Lalo swallowed hard.

Rosario nodded and stepped out onto the porch. When she saw the book in his hand, she made up her mind to something. "Leticia said to tell you good-bye," she said, her fingers crossed tightly behind her back. "She said she was sorry she had to go."

Lalo's unhappy face brightened. "She did?" he said again. He smiled to himself for a moment then held out the book. "Maybe you'd like to read this," he said. "It's called, *A Pearl for a Pauper.*"

"Sure," Rosario said. "Sure. I like books. But what's a 'pauper'?"

"A poor person."

"Pauper," she said slowly. "That's a funny word. You know an awful lot, don't you, Lalo?"

"Naw." He shrugged. "I just read a lot."

"Leticia does too," she said and was about to ask Lalo more about his book, but just then a panel truck turned into their driveway. It had a sign painted on its side: "Randy's. We Deliver."

The arrival of the truck was the second surprising thing that happened in that hour.

It stopped beside the elms and a stocky man in a tan uniform jumped out of the driver's seat. He looked at a clipboard in his hand. "Delivery for Rosario Silva. She live here?"

"That's me," Rosario said. "But what is it?"

"You'll have to open it to find out," the delivery man said with a smile. "But an adult has to sign for it first."

"I'll get my mother," Rosario said and ran into the house.

When Rosario and her mother came outside, there were two cartons on the porch. Lalo was bending over them.

"It's a computer," he said.

"But we didn't buy a computer," Mamá said. "Is it the right address? There must be a mistake."

The delivery man said, "There's a letter on the box."

Rosario pulled it off the carton and tore open the envelope. "Look," she said with surprise, "it's from Walgrove. Mamá! It's from Mr. Randolph, the man who owns the store those men were going to rob. He says the computer's for me! Like a reward, he says." She held the letter out to her mother.

Mamá read the letter through once, and then again more slowly. Finally, she said, "Well, if it's a gift, we can't very well return it," and signed the form.

The delivery man patted Lalo's shoulder. "I'll bet this young fellow will help you set it up."

"Sure," Lalo said, looking embarrassed, "if I can."

Rosario stared at Lalo. Is this Lalo the same one who's been picking on Jenny and me since we started middle school? "You would, really?" she said. "We'll do it together!"

"I suppose that will be all right," Mamá said, "but not today. Rosario's cousin just left and there are things we have to do. And Rosario will have to write a thank you note to Mr. Randolph."

Rosario had trouble holding back her disappointment. "Tomorrow, then?" she said. "Could you do it tomorrow, Lalo?"

"Hey," Lalo said, "tomorrow's cool. I'll be over about two-thirty."

Rosario said goodbye and rushed to the phone to call Jenny.

❖ ❖ ❖

True to his word, Lalo was at Rosario's house at exactly two-thirty on the following day. And so was Jenny. They came marching down the driveway at the same time, but not together, and Rosario was afraid that was a bad sign. Maybe they wouldn't talk to each other all afternoon. But when they saw the computer, things changed. They began talking as if there had never been any bad feelings between them.

The cartons had been opened the night before and the computer and printer were on the dining room table. Everyone in the family had had to take a look at them. Especially Rubén, who had a hard time hiding his chagrin because the new computer was a more powerful one than his. But now the computer was to go in Rosario's and Teresa's room, where they had made room for it between their beds.

By a quarter to four, Rosario had learned a few things about the wonderful machine she had been given. Still, she realized that there were a lot of questions that Lalo and Jenny and she couldn't answer, and for the first time in a long time she was glad that Rubén was her brother.

After Lalo and Jenny left, Rosario stared at the computer, not yet believing it was hers. She kept glancing at the clock, wondering when Rubén would get home. At five minutes after four she got up to ask Nina and Mamá about him. But the moment she stood up, pinpricks of guilt jabbed her. Leticia! She had forgotten her promise to Leticia!

She rushed to The Aerie. She sat on the bench and closed her eyes tightly. "Leticia," she whispered, "Leticia are you still there?" When above her in the branches a brown bird chirped and another chirped back, she relaxed. She was sure she had received an answer.

"Leticia," she said softly, "I'm sorry I was late, but it was because the greatest thing happened. Remember the store in Walgrove that the crooks were headed for? Well, the owner sent me a reward. And guess what it is? A computer! And guess who helped me set it up? Lalo. And Jenny. They're actually talking again. I thought that would never happen after

Jenny did what she did with his poem." Rosario bit her lip, sighed, and went on. "Guess I never told you about that. Well, it's not important now, 'cause it's all over. Looks like maybe the three of us are going to be friends, and I guess you had a lot to do with it, 'cause Lalo would never have come over, except to see you. Tomorrow, Jenny's going to bring over a game called, 'Beyond,' that Lalo says is neat. I'm sure it will be fun to play.

"Are you getting any of this, Leticia? I hope so." She stopped talking and in the quiet that followed listened for Leticia. When she heard the birds warbling again, she smiled and said, "There are two little brown birds singing away here in The Aerie. Remember when you named this place, you said the birds seemed to talk to you? Well, I'm taking their singing to mean that you're happier now that you're home. That absolutely has to be good. So I'm happier too. I didn't like it at all when you were sad."

Later that night, just before she fell asleep, Rosario thought back to talking to Leticia and, instead of feeling silly, she felt good. It had been nice—almost like having Leticia there.

❖ ❖ ❖

# Chapter Thirteen

Between the excitement of owning a computer and the magic of her meetings with Leticia in The Aerie, the days went by fast for Rosario. Both Jenny and Lalo spent a lot of time with her, practicing on the computer. And she wrote and printed her first letter to Leticia.

Of course, there was school, too. Lalo was still acting like a cool character with his friends and being a wise-cracker with his teachers, but he was okay with her. And right in the middle of the week, her poem was published in the school paper.

Before Rosario knew it, it was Thursday, exactly one week since Leticia had gone and the computer had arrived. At a little after four o'clock, Rosario was in The Aerie talking to Leticia about that.

"Leticia, it's been a whole week," she was saying in the under-her-breath voice that she thought of now as her "Aerie" voice. "You've been gone a whole week. You must really be glad to be home. Are you gaining any weight?

"I hope you got the letter I wrote you. I had fun putting in all those designs. The computer is wonderful. Wait till you see it! I guess you're back at school by now. Even though I really feel near to you here in The Aerie, I wish you'd write to me. It doesn't have to be a long letter. A little one would be okay. All right. Now I'll be quiet and just sit here and let you talk to me."

Rosario sat back, closed her eyes, and listened to the faraway sounds: the drone of an airplane high in the sky; a little clang and clatter as Nina dropped something in the kitchen; the soft rustle of dry branches as a breeze began; and then, clear and beautiful from beyond the brick fence, the bell-like tone of their neighbor's wind chimes.

She opened her eyes. That had to be a message from Leticia. She grinned. In any case, she'd pretend that it was. She sat on the bench listening to the sounds for a little while longer and then went into the house.

"Where have you been, girl?" Nina asked when she stepped into the kitchen. "Here, help me peel these potatoes."

Rosario grinned at her grandmother. "You don't even have to ask, do you, Nina? You know where I've been. You know a lot of things."

"What I know best," Nina said, "is when to listen and say nothing."

Right after supper that night, Rosario and Teresa washed the dishes and then went in to watch TV. When the telephone rang, they both looked up expectantly. Papá answered it as usual.

His face was serious as he listened, then he nodded and said to Mamá, "Pick up the phone in the bedroom, Mela. This call is for you and Nina Sara, too."

Mamá and Nina stayed in the bedroom for a long time. Finally, along with Papá, they came into the living room. Mamá had her arm around Nina's shoulders, and both of them had tears in their eyes.

"Turn off the television, girls," Papá said.

Teresa, whose eyes had never left the TV screen, muttered, "You're making us miss the best part." But one look at her father and she quickly pressed the off-button on the remote.

Rosario stared at her mother and an icy little fear raced up her spine. It wasn't strange to see tears in Mamá's eyes. She even cried at sad things on TV. But Nina? Nina never cried. Something was very wrong. What? What? And then she knew.

"It's Leticia," she said, "isn't it? Is she worse?"

"Yes," Mamá said, "it's Leticia." She sat by Rosario's side and took her hand. "But it's more than that, mi'jita. Leticia has..." Mamá shook her head and sighed. "Leticia died today."

Teresa muttered, "Oh, god, that's awful."

Rosario jumped up and faced her mother. She stood before her, hands clenched into fists, her breath coming fast. "That's a lie!" she cried. "A big lie! Leticia's getting better. That's why the doctors sent her home!" Tears started and streamed down her cheeks and into the corners of her mouth. They tasted salty. Angrily, she rubbed the back of her hand across her mouth. She whirled around, raced from the room and out of the house.

It was deeply dark below the elms. For a moment she pressed against the trunk of the nearest tree, then pushed away and ran to The Aerie. There she cried until she could cry no more. She sat listening to the quiet night as her sobs lessened. Her thoughts were not quiet. They were screaming that Mamá had to be wrong. Another part of her whispered that she was wrong.

It was common sense talking to her heart, and her heart didn't want to listen. Even so, she knew it was true. Leticia had died. Leticia was gone. Gone. No matter where you looked, Leticia would not be there. Not in Kelton, not in Los Angeles, not hiding in a grove of trees in Walgrove. Leticia would never be there. Leticia was gone. She sighed, a long shivering sigh, and leaned against the brick fence.

In a little while she heard the back door open and Nina's voice saying, "Let the child be. She's all right."

And then she was alone with the night once more. Through an open space in the shrubs she stared up at the sky. An airplane's safety light blinked down at her and she said softly, "That's not a star, dummy, that's an airplane."

Above Rosario a little breeze rustled the dry leaves.

❖ ❖ ❖

# Chapter Fourteen

Even with a cup of hot milk and honey that Nina fixed for her before bedtime, Rosario did not sleep well that night. Her dreams were weird, and she awakened tired and unhappy.

She dreaded to go back to school. She was sure that with just one look everyone would know that something terrible had happened to her. But she found that no one noticed anything. Not even Jenny.

"Hi," Jenny said when she saw her. "My dad has a computer program called, 'Reach,' that he says..."

"Jenny," Rosario interrupted, "Leticia died."

"What?"

"I said Leticia died. Yesterday."

"Oh," Jenny said, "that's terrible. But how?"

"She was very sick."

"All this time?" Jenny frowned. "Oh. Is that why she kept coming here?"

"Yes," Rosario said, "she had cancer."

Jenny opened her mouth to say something and closed it again. They walked silently to their first-period class.

At the end of the school day, she waited for Lalo by his locker. "Lalo," she said when he showed up, "I've got something to tell you."

"Sure," Lalo said. "Shoot."

Rosario swallowed hard. "Leticia died," she said. "Yesterday. Up in Kelton where she lives. She was very sick."

Lalo turned his back and rummaged in his locker. He said something, she didn't know what, then he slammed the locker door shut and walked away.

"Lalo," she called after him, "what're you doing? What's wrong?"

Nina was the only one who went to Kelton for Leticia's funeral. There had been much discussion about whether or not Papá's car could make it over the mountains into the Central Valley so that everyone in the family could go. Then, when that was voted against, there had been talk about the high cost of airplane tickets.

Because it was Saturday, Rosario was able to go with her father and mother to take Nina to the airport. When Nina's flight number was called, Rosario watched her disappear into the tunnel-like passage and wanted to cry, "Don't go!" Everyone is leaving me!

No one talked much on the way home. But when they got there and Rosario said, "I think I'll stay out here a while," Papá smiled at her and gave her an extra-tight hug.

Rosario walked to the edge of the driveway, waved to Mr. Milliken, and returned to the house. At the bottom of the front steps, she paused. There was something new on the porch. A small rosebush in a clay planting pot was at the top of the steps. The bush was covered with glistening green leaves and it had five dainty pink roses.

A note on the edge of the pot said, "For Rosario. This rose is called 'Pink Beauty.' Plant it in the sun, give it love and care, and it will bloom for many years. If you need help with it, you know where I am. Your friend, Mr. M."

Rosario put the note down and looked again at the flowers. They were the same dusty pink that Leticia always wore. She was sure that Mr. Milliken had known that.

Her mother was standing on the other side of the screen door. Rosario said, "Mr. Milliken sent me this. I know just where it should go. May I plant it?"

Mamá nodded. "By your special place? There's a good spot there. Do you want some help?"

Rosario shook her head. "I think I can do it." She picked up the clay pot and took it around the house and across the back yard. She had just finished prying the rosebush out of its pot with a trowel when the back door opened.

"Rosario," Mamá called. "Jenny wants to know if she can come over. Do you want to talk to her?"

"Tell her to come over, please."

Although the soil was soft, digging a hole big enough for her plant was not an easy job. It was barely started when Jenny arrived.

"I brought Leticia's pictures," she said as she came down the back steps. "What're you doing?"

"Planting a rose. To remember Leticia by. I think that's why Mr. Milliken gave it to me."

"Oh," Jenny said, "and you'll have the pictures too. I left them in the house. I'll go get them."

Before Jenny had returned, Lalo appeared around the corner of the house. "Your sister said you were back here," he said. "What're you doing?"

"Planting a rose. To remember Leticia by."

Lalo looked at the rosebush for a long time. "It's pink," he said finally. "It's pretty. Do you want me to help you?"

"I want to help too," Jenny called from the back door.

"Sure," Rosario said. "We'll all do it." She handed Lalo the spade.

Lalo dug the hole deeper. Jenny brought the hose over and filled the bottom with water. Carefully, Rosario picked up the plant.

"The five pink roses haven't wilted at all," she said.

Then the three of them on their knees eased the rose into the newly dug earth and patted the wet ground around it.

Rosario smiled at her friends then looked at the little bush. She would take good care of it as long as it lasted.